Paris

Paris

Edited by
Andrew Hodgson

Dostoyevsky Wannabe Cities
An Imprint of Dostoyevsky Wannabe

First Published in 2019
by Dostoyevsky Wannabe Cities
All rights reserved
© All copyright reverts to individual authors

Dostoyevsky Wannabe Cities is an imprint of
Dostoyevsky Wannabe publishing.

www.dostoyevskywannabe.com

This anthology is a work of fiction. The names, characters and incidents portrayed in it are the work of the authors' imagination. Any resemblance to actual persons, living or dead, events or localities is entirely coincidental.

Cover design by Dostoyevsky Wannabe Design

ISBN-9781072051930

Dostoyevsky Wannabe Cities books represent a snapshot of the writing of a particular locale at a particular moment in time. The content is reflective of the choices of the guest-editor.

No parts of this publication may be reproduced, stored in a retrieval system, or transmitted in any form or by any means, electronic, mechanical, photocopying, recording, or otherwise, without the prior written permission of the copyright owner.

This book is sold subject to the condition that it shall not, by way of trade or otherwise, be lent, resold, hired out, or otherwise circulated without the publisher's prior consent in any form of binding or cover other than that in which it is published and without a similar condition including this condition being imposed on the subsequent purchaser. Under no circumstances may any part of this book be photocopied for resale.

Contents

Intros/Outros	7
Craig Dworkin	9
Lauren Elkin	17
Gaia Di Lorenzo	29
Olivier Salon & Chris Clarke	41
Yelena Moskovich	59
Camille Bloomfield	69
Stewart Home	81
Amalie Brandt	93
Ian Monk	97
Andrew Gallix	105
Eric Giraudet De Boudemange	121
Andrew Hodgson	131
Philipp Timischl	139
Contributors	143

INTROS/OUTROS

The book, its contents, that follows is product of a theme, of language as physical, ephemeral, medium – of spoken, written, language as object locked in constant interacting processes of the generative and the disintegratory.

With Paris as physical place, as disseminated cultural construct, as environment in which French – Franglais, Frenglish, English et al. is spoken, written, and with which humans attempt to interact. With physical, ephemeral, space of interaction centred here as a series of wide-ranging content-form writerly, projected readerly, treatments of language, of lingual experience, of experiential communication. Successive, successful, warped – broken, and/or falling into failure operations of art, literary, mediations of a central theme, of. Dostoyevsky Wannabe Cities *Paris* – interacting, interactions of, with, within, language as object, as medium.

Andrew Hodgson
Paris, 30 April 2019

CRAIG DWORKIN
From *DEF*

Process Note: Following a proposal that Raymond Queneau called "definitional literature," which had a precedent in Stefan Themerson's "semantic literature" and which was taken up most fully by Georges Perec and Marcel Bénabou, I began with a sentence from Gottlob Frege and replaced each of the words in his text with its dictionary definition. I then replaced each of the words in that new sentence with its dictionary definition, and then each of the words in that new sentence *its* dictionary definition, and so on. The following presents one of the resulting elaborations.

"*On the introduction of a name for something simple, a definition is not possible; there is nothing for it but to lead the reader or hearer, by means of hints, to understand the words as is intended.*"[1]

By which I mean: with reference to, as regards, or, strictly speaking: concerning, about the something that is done or performed, a deed, an act of bringing (a thing) into some sphere of action or thought, or, in other words: bringing in in the course of some action or in a literary or artistic composition, or, *id est*: adding or inserting as a feature or element, sometimes with the notion of bringing in for the first time or as a new feature, a conducing or

1 Gottlob Frege: "On Concept and Object," Trans. P. T. Geach and Max Black, *Mind* (Vol. 60, No. 238, April, 1951): 168-180.

fetching in, a carrying into the act of putting something to work, or employing or applying a thing, for any (especially a beneficial or productive) purpose or the actual application or use of an idea, belief, or method, as opposed to the theory or principles of it, conducing or fetching in in the natural exercise of the vocal organs, or, expressly: the utterance of words or sentences, or, *scilicet*: oral expression of thought or feeling or the penning or forming of letters or words, the action of setting or putting in, the introduction into or between of a word used as the name or designation of a person, place, or thing suitable for a specified or implicit purpose or requirement, or, particularly: appropriate to the circumstances or conditions, or, expressly: of the requisite standard or type, or, to wit: apt, fitting, or, *videlicet*: correct, right, a speech, utterance, verbal expression or a small group or collocation of words expressing a single notion, or entering with some degree of unity into the structure of a sentence, or, that is: a common or idiomatic expression making up, forming, composing the indivisible act of marking or pointing out by which a role or character assumed in real life, or in a play, or that which is stated or expressed in speech, writing, etc., or, in plain English: a saying, an utterance, an expression, a statement that is a unit or one among a number, taken or considered apart from the rest, is publicly identified as such, concerned with, or written and sent for some unspecified or not definitely set down matter (earthly or spiritual) with which one is concerned with nothing increased, in other words, taken into account, or transferred by one's own direct act (a thing) into one's possession or keeping, to be appropriated by its own, in other words: a sheet of standing water, free from contamination or physical impurity, or, strictly speaking: not mixed with anything that corrupts or impairs, or, by way of explanation: untainted, clean, unclothed, naked, nude, that is to say: unaccompanied or unsupported by others, or, *i.e.*, alone, solitary, a formal written or oral account of facts, theories, opinions, events, characterized by definiteness or exactness of expression of the inherent dominating power or impulse in a person by which character or action is determined, directed, or controlled in the highest sense of a deliberative or judicial assembly is not among the strengths of an individual human being, or, in plain English, a man, woman, or child; there is not any (physical substance or incorporeal) sake for it but to go with (a person) as a companion, escort, or attendant and bring forward or display a track prepared or available for travelling along in order that it may be looked at, in other words: to inform, instruct, or guide or go with or before for the purpose of leading the way (said of persons, of God, Providence, and of impersonal agents, such as stars, light, etc.) by walking on in a step forward in other words, to speak familiarly, converse, talk, chat to go or come after in one's way or track formed by the continued treading of pedestrians or animals, rather than one deliberately planned and made, or, namely: a narrow unmade and (usually) unenclosed way that people on foot can use an expositor or official or professional expounder of laws, texts, mysteries, etc., or, *scilicet*: a commentator of a train of thoughts, images, or fancies passing through the mind during sleep, gestures or motion used to convey information or instructions of or relating to magic, alchemy, astrology, theosophy, or other practical arts held to involve agencies of a secret or mysterious nature, etc., or one who learns by oral instruction, by a contrivance for producing musical sounds, by the vibrations of some solid material (as strings, reeds, rods, membranes, etc.), or of a body of air in a pipe or tube, or some mediation, some recommended or prescribed medical treatment for a specific disease, or a gallop on horseback of a gesture in oratory or dramatic performance devoted to come so near as to touch some something placed before or presented to the eyes or other senses or to accomplish some effect, consequence, or outcome of some action, process, or design of slender suggestions stretched out to be captured by those having a high degree or good measure of understanding, or, in other words: promptings or incitements to evil or entwinings, or entanglings accompanied in token of courtesy or honour in a crooked, devious or concealed, hidden, secret distinct type or kind, to seize, grasp, lay hold of, catch, that is to say: to take down, in writing, the moaning, lamentation or that which a thing (especially a document, phrase, word, etc.) involves, implies, betokens, or indicates in other words, to make clutches with the hand at the abstract or eternally existing pattern or archetype of any kind of thing (in Platonic philosophy), in relation to which particular things are conceived as imperfect copies or approximations, and often as deriving their existence from it, of a quantity or number however great or small of the manner in which the tense of a subordinate clause depends on that of the principal clause of a single or individual or greater in number, sensation or sensations produced in the organs of hearing when the surrounding air is set in vibration in such a way as to affect these or the grammatical elements (acknowledged, accepted, or, namely: known, identified by direct and immediate vision by direct, straightforward, literal orators as) ordaining the fundamental determinate quantities, dimensions, or magnitudes adopted as a basis or standard of measurement for other quantities of the same kind and in terms of which their magnitudes are calculated or expressed of the natural exercise of the vocal organs compatible with the rules of a logical language or other sign system customarily employed, experienced, or encountered in moulding a way of thinking or a degree which surpasses bounds or goes beyond measure in respect of severity, vehemence, etc., or, in other words: immoderate force or violence in a system of spoken or written communication used by a particular country, people, community, etc., typically consisting of words used within a regular grammatical and syntactic structure (and in a larger proportion of the whole of an organized or connected group of objects engaged in, addicted to, writing as a rule set apart or asunder, disjoined, withdrawn, by time which is free or available for doing something, or, in plain English, leisure, or, *id est*: opportunity) in other words, single individuals or things regarded as members of a group or number of things or individuals, or discriminated from these as having a separate existence pertaining or relating to the words or vocabulary of a language other than particular choices or combinations of words used to express an idea, sentiment, etc., in an effective manner, or, especially: striking or pithy expressions, or, in other words: also occasionally: meaningless, trite, or high-sounding forms of words or appendages, that is to say: statements, maxims, or admonitions such as were commonly introduced by the word *item* of a collection or list of words with brief explanations of their meanings, names or designations, as is proffered to be performed, executed, accomplished, finished, ended, settled, or, *id est*: also, used up, worn out or brought to an end, in other words: marked out, appointed, designated, intended, *id est*: marked out, appointed, designated to be what is stated in writing by the word used as the name or designation of a person, place, or thing in other words, performed, executed, accomplished, finished, ended, settled, or, *id est*: also, used up, worn out on that which forms or ought to form the subject of a discourse, or, *viz.*: the matter in hand, or, especially: the point at issue, applied by some to the use of the Future or Imperfect tense, in other words: prostrated away from a central or inner point, or from a point of origin or onwards from a specified point, or, *scilicet*: continuously in one direction, or, by way of explanation: without deviation or interruption, distended, enlarged, in other words: buried at full length, in other words: the waxing in violence or 'stress' of weather or the high-strung quality of personal feeling or emotion, employed or interpreted in a laboured, far-fetched, or non-natural sense, or, expressly: wrested or distorted from the natural meaning or intention, or, especially: pressed, forced, pushed beyond what is natural or reasonable.

LAUREN ELKIN
I am a French Novelist

At the Forum of the Book, in the eastern part of the country, I sit between two piles of a novel I have recently published, and try to look nonchalant while people walk past me on their way to other writers sitting between slowly diminishing stacks of their own books. Next to me sit other writers from my publisher. François to my right. Christian to my left. They, too, play the game. Poker face. Or friendly face. Christian energetically hands out bookmarks.

An elderly woman uses my books to lean on. I want to offer her something, a sip of water, my chair, but she moves on. "She'll be dead soon anyway," says François. François likes to speak English. "One foot in the grave and the other sleeping," he tells me. I puzzle this out for a minute and realize he means "slipping," not sleeping. One foot in the grave and the other slipping.

Everyone is very specific about how they set up their books. They put a couple facing out and space them evenly. They create a mosaic of their old and new books. I only have the one. I leave it in stacks. The tablecloths -

pale blue - have written on them *Hopitaux Universitaires de Sud Alsace*.

This kind of book fair, I am learning, is a necessary ritual when you publish a book in France. The French version of a book tour. François and I have been to a bunch of them this past spring, in Geneva, in Nancy, in Brittany. Each place has its own local charms; each group of people their own concerns. Now here we are in a small-ish town in Alsace. Dinner, tonight, is meant to take place at the local casino.

I'm in the awkward position of having published a book in French that I wrote in English without the book having appeared in English. Sitting next to my book in French, while speaking French that marks me out as a non-native, is confusing to people. Where can they buy it in English, they ask, these brilliant people who would rather read me in my native language. I feel great affection for them for their enthusiasm, and serious dismay that I can't fulfill it. I have already begun writing my next novel in French and in English, letting each section emerge as it will, translating it back the other way. It takes twice as long. But the extra work is a normal part of living in this liminal position, between two languages, between two cultures. Most things take twice as long.

François discusses the upcoming presidential elections

with an older man in a tracksuit, who wonders if Hollande has a chance against the Sarkozy machine. He asks us, visitors to his provincial town, what the atmosphere is like in Paris. "It's different in the metro now people seem less inclined to want to beat each other up," François offers. They are both happy DSK didn't make it in, not because of that rape thing but because of his lack of intellectual credentials. "He's known to be an economist but as an academic he never published anything," Tracksuit says. "No proof of" François replies, and I tune out, because I can do that, tune out the French, not understand if I no longer want to understand.

I make eye contact with one of the authors across the way, who is selling a book about Patagonia. I smile. She smiles. We look away again.

A young man comes by and picks up my book. He's not going to buy it, I think. Venice, love story, lady writer, he's not going to buy it. I'm right. He moves on.
Another young man comes by. This one actually opens the book. "You're American," he says. "What do you think of Obama?" He does not buy the book, though I tell him how much I love Obama.

Another young man comes by, turns the book around, opens it, closes it. "You're American," he says. "Why did you write this book in French?"

"I didn't," I say. "I wrote it in English and someone translated it into French." I have a flashback to sitting up one night reading the translation for the first time. Howling at the howlers. In one scene, set at a party, I wrote: "Nirvana blares from the speakers. Here we are now. Entertain us." Or something to that effect. The translator's offering: "Every word from the people's mouths as they speak is nirvana." The lyrics he simply cut. I start to tell the story but he waves me off and moves on.

Looking around at all the writers sitting hopefully by their stacks, I wonder if they will all find their readers. And these just the ones at this book fair. So many others, across the country. Seven hundred novels published every rentrée. And that's just in this country. What justifies it all? I think of something Samuel Johnson wrote about the proliferation of books, year after year: "The cause, therefore, of this epidemical conspiracy for the destruction of paper, must remain a secret…" Johnson lived before people worried about the anthropocene, climate change, deforestation. Should we all be reading e-books, to save on paper? However would we hawk *those* at a book fair?

I have no idea how to make people buy my book. My

editor's husband strides by looking serious but this is probably a cover for how drunk he already is at three in the afternoon. Over lunch the other writers on my imprint were worrying because we are very strangely not getting the foot traffic we ought to, considering we're in the central row. The crowds seem to split right before our booth, flowing off in opposite directions, pulled by minor literary celebrities at either end. I feel naive for publishing a novel, and not for the first time.

I get a text from François, who is sitting next to me pretending to be answering emails on his phone. *I want to see you naked.*
There are a lot of children here. I should write children's books. My friend just made a pile of money from writing a children's book. And at least then it would seem less nakedly - god that word, no, less *transparently* - self-serving. It wouldn't be for glory and self-expression, it would be for the children.

I feel embarrassed about the come-hither-and-read author photo suspended above my head. As if I were sitting here because my publisher decided I was pretty and that would help sell the book. As if the guys on either side of me were real writers whereas I'm just a blond.
A nice-looking middle aged woman picks up my book, readers the back for what feels like ages. I put my phone down so as not to look like one of those smartphone

addicts (I am one though) and try to do something productive that doesn't involve staring at her or waiting blankly for her to buy it or not. I take a drink of water and neaten Christian's bookmarks. She puts the book down and walks away.

"You have to talk to them!" François says. "Watch me."

It's kind of embarrassing to be the author of a book with a gondola on the cover.

People seem to like the Patagonia book. The author stands and talks to people.

Some people have brought their dogs with them to the book fair. You hear yelps as people step on them, or barking and scrabbling as they get into fights.

A woman approaches a writer and asks: "Who is Valérie d'Eguisheim?" The author answers: "I am." "Why are you called Valérie d'Eguisheim?" Valérie doesn't miss a beat. "Because that's my name!" "Are you from Eguisheim?" Valérie grants that once upon a time, yes, her family must have been, historically speaking. "So then why do you mispronounce your name?" The woman, who is from Alsace, cannot understand it. She heard Valérie on the radio, mispronouncing her own name. It should be pronounced German-ly, "Eguishaim," not French-ly, "Eguishehm."

There are no Russians around to debate the pronunciation of my last name. The French, however, are happy to correct me every time I say it, no matter how I say it. Half of them believe it should be pronounced "Elk-ihn," nasally, whereas I tend to pronounce it, when speaking French, as "Elkeen." The few times I've tried to go the other way, someone gently informs me that the *i* is long, not short, because it's not a French name, as if I had been trying to pass myself off as French.

Word goes around that Nancy Huston will imminently give a talk. "I used to read Nancy Huston," I hear a man say. "Then I stopped taking drugs." The talk begins. A woman listens, curious to hear what Huston's French sounds like. "She has a weird accent," the woman announces. "That's not Nancy Huston!" says the man with her. "That woman is German."

I try smiling at people. Some smile back. But it doesn't make them come over. I try ignoring people. They ignore me back. That doesn't make them come over either. "You're not very good at this, are you," says my editor's husband.

I think about reading the book I've brought with me, Dany Laferrière's *Je suis un écrivain japonais*, then think I might not look serious enough if I'm seen reading someone else's book, published by some other publisher. I like the way he jettisons the whole idea of writing and nationality out the window. Born in Haiti in 1953, Laferrière moved to Canada in 1976. He writes in French, and soon after this book fair would be elected to the Académie Française, to safeguard the French language for at least a generation. But none of that matters. I'm a Japanese writer, he says, absurdly.

I want people to stop and buy my books but I'd be happy if they just stopped by and picked them up so I wouldn't have to sit here trying not to stare blankly into space, or fending off François's salty texts.

Someone picks up my book, asks me if it's available in English, I say no, they move on.

François comes back from the bathroom where he has had an altercation with someone. He's in rare form. He tells me what he would have said to the person in English if the person spoke English: *Suck my duck, punk. Muzzuhfuckah beetch. Rape my bread.* His English is more creative than mine could ever be. I tell him he should think about becoming an English writer.

Toward the end of the afternoon they offer us cheap wine in plastic cups and pretzels. A woman recommends that I visit Chioggia next time I'm in Venice.

Later that evening back at the hotel we have some drinks and play some pool. My skirt is short and when I lean over to make a shot my editor's husband grabs my ass. I hit him on the head with my pool cue but he just laughs. François laughs. A little old man with round glasses laughs. There are no other women in the room.

The next day I have a hangover from drinking too much Alsatian champagne. At breakfast they asked me if I wanted des eaux. What? I couldn't compute. *Egg*, the woman spits out, in hard English. Oh des *oeufs*.

François comes by my table to complain. "Oh, fuck a dwarf," he complains.

I chat to a writer who stops by the stand, wearing a t-shirt that says *Daddy don't bullshit me*. Along comes a young man wearing a t-shirt that says *running sucks*. They commiserate. Neither one buys a book.

Later that morning I'm on a panel called écrivains britanniques, despite not being a British writer. On my panel is Stephen Clarke, who reveals that it's in his contract that every book he publishes has to have the word merde in it. I find this very depressing.

On the panel is another American woman who is also not a British writer. The moderator is convinced that all aspects of her novel as well as my own are based on autobiographical fact.

After the panel, I walk around. I meet a Scottish writer, whom I immediately love. We talk about the new book I'm writing, which is about walking. She tells me about stravaigin, Gaelic for a purposeful walk without a goal, and about the fact that there's no possessive in Gaelic — you don't own the drink, the drink is with you. You don't own the land, the land is with you. She's about to get married, she tells me. Tradition Gaelic marriage was for 3-7 years, she says, renewable if mutually agreed-upon.

Back at my stand I talk to a woman whose sixteen year-old daughter has self-published a book set in medieval Jerusalem — her author photo shows her clad in a green velvet medieval gown, perched atop a horse. Several people walk by carrying stacks of books under their arms. Stacks! Like at least ten books! I am encouraged. Ils achètent, ces gens-ci, mutters François.
Douglas Kennedy is doing a brisk business, of course. I open Dany Laferrière.

Soon after a little girl picks up my book. "Hello!" I say to her in English with a bright smile. She runs away and hides her face in her father's leg.

Someone who's overheard the woman telling me about her sixteen year-old asks me the difference between being published by a publisher or being self-published. I stammer out an explanation that seems redundant. Which is better? He asks. I check to make sure the woman is no longer within earshot. I'm answering for myself, of course, not for her daughter. Well, I say. Someone pays you to publish your book, versus you pay to publish it yourself. I guess the first one? He shrugs.

By the time we return to Paris, I've sold eight books in all. I don't know how many they expected me to sell but this seems not terrible, considering I probably don't sell eight books a day when I'm not at a festival. I make a mental note to bring some bookmarks, next time. And to wear trousers.

GAIA DI LORENZO

- Eh bien, je risquerai d'abord, avant de commencer, deux propositions. Elles paraîtront, elles aussi, incomposibles. Non seulement contradictoires en elles-mêmes, cette fois, mais contradictoires entre elles. Elles prennent la forme d'une loi, chaque fois une loi. Le rapport d'antagonisme que ces deux lois entretiennent chaque fois entre elles, tu l'appelleras donc, si tu aimes ce mot que j'aime, antinomie. - Soit. Quelles seraient donc ces deux propositions ? Je t'écoute. - Les voici: 1. On ne parle jamais qu'une seule langue. 2. On ne parle jamais une seule langue.

Rien n'est intraduisible en un sens, mais en un autre sens tout est intraduisible, la traduction est un autre nom de l'impossible. En un autre sens du mot « traduction », bien sûr, et d'un sens à l'autre il m'est facile de tenir toujours ferme entre ces deux hyperboles qui sont au fond la même et se traduisent encore l'une l'autre.

Jacques Derrida, Monolingualism of the Other, or Prosthesis of Origin (pp. 7, 57)

Un syllogisme:
Rien n'est intraduisible.
Tout est intraduisible.
Rien est tout.

Translation is quite something

In my own work I find that language is always changing me as much as I change it – that it is recreating me as I rework and reshape it. This is as much a feeling as it is a philosophy. Still, translation, under Nietzsche-cum-Malabou's plastic paradigm, is itself an act of re-creation. It is always making something out of something, not something out of nothing. […] The brain adapts to change and also changes what happens next. Each time we carry out an activity it is repeated but also altered by the differences within the experience.

Allison Grimaldi-Donahue, Poetry's Intrinsic Ontology of Change
http://www.publicseminar.org/2018/05poetrys-intrinsic-ontology-of-change/, May 2018

It is always making something out of something, not something out of nothing.
Nothing is out of nothing. But that's positive!

Ho sceso, dandoti il braccio…

Ho sceso, dandoti il braccio, almeno un milione di scale
e ora che non ci sei è il vuoto ad ogni gradino.
Anche così è stato breve il nostro lungo viaggio.
Il mio dura tuttora, né più mi occorrono
le coincidenze, le prenotazioni,
le trappole, gli scorni di chi crede
che la realtà sia quella che si vede.
Ho sceso milioni di scale dandoti il braccio
non già perché con quattr'occhi forse si vede di più.
Con te le ho scese perché sapevo che di noi due
le sole vere pupille, sebbene tanto offuscate,
erano le tue.

di Eugenio Montale, "Satura", 1971

No, non ho mai sceso dandoti il braccio.
e ora che ci sei, è il vuoto a ogni gradino.

How long will our journey last?
Guarda che lo so che il mio solitario durerà ancora,
oltre le nostre coincidenze Tomm, le nostre prenotazioni
e lo scorno di chi crede
che la realtà è quella che si vede.

Voglio scendere dandoti il braccio
non già perché con quattr'occhi forse si vede di più
Con te le voglio scendere solo perché (just because).

Albus Dumbledore: Harry, you wonderful boy. You brave man. Let us walk.

Harry Potter: Professor, what is that?

Albus Dumbledore: Something beyond either of our help. A part of Voldemort, sent here to die.

Harry Potter: And exactly where are we?

Albus Dumbledore: I was going to ask you that. Where would you say that we are?

Harry Potter: Well, it looks like King's Cross Station, only cleaner, and without all the trains.

Albus Dumbledore: King's Cross, is that right? This is, as they say, your party. I expect you now realize that you and Voldemort have been connected by something other than fate, since that night in Godric's Hollow all those years ago.

Harry Potter: So it's true then, isn't it, Sir? A part of him lives in me, doesn't it?

Albus Dumbledore: Did. It was just destroyed many moments ago by none other than Voldemort himself. You were the Horcux he never meant to make, Harry.

[They sit on a bench]

Harry Potter: I have to go back, haven't I?

Albus Dumbledore: Oh, that's up to you.

Harry Potter: I have a choice?

Albus Dumbledore: Oh, yes. We're in King's Cross, you say? I think if you so desired, you'd be able to board a train.

Harry Potter: And where would it take me?

Albus Dumbledore: [chuckles] On.

[Dumbledore begins walking away]

Harry Potter: Voldemort has the Elder Wand.

Albus Dumbledore: True.

Harry Potter: And the snake's still alive.

Albus Dumbledore: Yes.

Harry Potter: And I've nothing to kill it with.

Albus Dumbledore: [walks back to Harry] Help will always be given at Hogwarts, Harry, to those who ask for it. I've always prized myself on my ability to turn a phrase. Words are, in my not so humble opinion, our most inexhaustible source of magic. Capable of both inflicting injury, and remedying it.But I would, in this case, amend my original statement to this: "Help would always be given at Hogwarts to those who deserve it." Do not pity the dead, Harry. Pity the living. And above all, those who live without love.

Harry Potter: Professor, my mother's Patronus was a doe, wasn't it? It's the same as Professor Snape's. It's curious, don't you think?

Albus Dumbledore: Actually, if I think about it, it doesn't seem curious at all. I'll be going now, Harry. [turns to leave]

Harry Potter: Professor? Is this all real? Or is it just happening inside my head?

Albus Dumbledore: Of course it's happening inside

your head, Harry. Why should that mean that it's not real? [he fades into the light]
Harry Potter: Professor, what shall I do? Professor?

Harry Potter and the Deathly Hallows, J.K. Rowling

Of course it's happening inside your head, Harry. Why should that mean that it's not real?

OLIVIER SALON & CHRIS CLARKE

What happens to a text when its author is aware of its impending translation? Can a text be aware of its own translation? Can the original communicate with its translation-counterpart? Olivier Salon and I decided to explore these questions. My goal in translating a text is to share my reading of it with new readers, to preserve the effect the text had on me when I read it. But here, I had to ask an important question: who will be able to read my translation in a way similar to how I read Olivier's text?

I decided the only solution was to translate this text for the same audience as it was written: a translator of constrained literature like me. The resulting text functions in English much as it did in Olivier's French, or as close as the differences between our languages allow. The challenges within have been maintained for two more translators, each asked to translate my English text back to French. These colleagues are both trilingual, and I've asked them to translate our text into French, but, rather than focusing on the problems that lie between English and French, to consider those between French and their third languages. The solutions will be their own and dictated by their text and language pairs, as the translator for whom they set their traps awaits them behind a distinct system of incompatibilities.

If our opening discussions conjured up a text that would be in some way completed by its translation, the result turns out to have been the opposite: a text that will forever remain open, that must continue on in perpetuity into different personal variations and linguistic combinations. I look forward to seeing the next iterations of this text, wherever it might end up.

Chris Clarke, April 2019

Étant donnés un auteur, un traducteur
et le gaz d'éclairage
ou *Comment déjouer les tours de Babel ?*

Olivier Salon, pour Chris Clarke

Les écrivains que je connais et qui me connaissent prétendent que je suis un auteur intraduisible. Un auteur intraduisible.

Les textes que j'écris, disent-ils en effet, sont trop truffés de jeux de mots, de variations homophoniques ou de jeux de langue française pour qu'un traducteur puisse risquer d'y faire son

travail convenablement.

Pourtant, ici ou là, certains textes, que j'ai seulement pensés en langue française, ont été depuis traduits : *S'exercer*, sonnet monovocalique (la seule voyelle autorisée y est le *e*) autodescriptif,

a été traduit par Rachel Galvin, sous le titre *Exert*. Ce sonnet présentait, outre les difficultés inhérentes à la traduction monovocalique, quelques astuces supplémentaires et non des moindres. Ainsi, Pierre Corneille écrit-il dans Polyeucte le célèbre vers :

Given an Author, a Translator, and Gas-lighting, or
*How One's Wit
May Tower So High as to Thwart Babel*

Olivier Salon for Chris Clarke,
for Camille Bloomfield & Santiago Artozqui

Writers whom Olivier Salon knows and who know him claim that he is an untranslatable author. An untranslatable author.

The texts he writes, these people are effectively saying, are riddled with too many puns, too much homophonic variation or wordplay specific to the French language for a translator to run the risk of applying to them his usual methodology.

And yet, now and again, certain texts that he had conceived of exclusively in French have since been translated: "S'exercer," a self-describing monovocalic (in which the only permitted vowel is an *e*) sonnet, was translated by Rachel Galvin, and given the title "S' Exert." Apart from the difficulties inherent to monovocalic translation, this sonnet presented several additional puns, and not of the simplest nature. In his "Polyeucte," Pierre Corneille similarly penned a famous line, which I might translate as:

« Et le désir s›accroît quand **l'effet se recule**. »
On peut le lire tel quel, mais on peut entendre :
« Et le désir s›accroît quand **les fesses reculent**. »
Or, j'ai moi-même fait un clin d'œil à Corneille en écrivant dans mon sonnet *S'exercer* :
« Redresse tes pensées et sens **l'effet se tendre**
      Pénètre ces secrets… »
ce qui peut s'entendre ainsi :
« Redresse tes pensées et sens les fesses tendres
Pénètre ces secrets… »

Voilà des jeux de mots typiquement français, jouant sur l'homophonie, que Chris Clarke ne pourrait en aucune façon traduire.

Sardinosaures (qui combine *sardine* et *dinosaure* en un mot-valise) a été partiellement traduit en italien par Eliana Vicari sous le titre *I sardinosauri*. Cela peut sembler simple de prime abord, mais la traductrice a bien dû trouver un équivalent pour le *Vautourterelle*, le *Homarcassin* ou la *Truître*. Que ferait un traducteur anglais de son côté ? Ou encore avec *l'Escargoéland* que voici :

"And desire, how it swells when **her ear is pressed close.**"
Which we can read as it is written, but we can also hear:
"And desire, how it swells when **her rear is pressed close.**"
Similarly, Olivier was giving Corneille a wink when he wrote, in his sonnet, which I'm now translating as "S' Excellence":
"See them embers well, feel **her tender ere end,**
Enter the deepest secrets…"
Which can also be heard in this way:
"See them embers well, feel **her tender rear end,**
Enter the deepest secrets…"
These are two examples of wordplay typical to French that employ homophony of the
sort that Olivier thought I would be completely unable to translate.

"Sardinosaurs" (which combines *sardine* and *dinosaur* in a portmanteau word) was first partially translated from French into Italian by Eliana Vicari, under the title "I sardinosauri." It may seem simple at first, but a translator also needs to find an equivalent for "The Vulturtledove," "The Craboon" or "The Albatrout." What will another translator do with these in his or her own tongue? And what about with "The Hipposprey," which is here:

> Avec ses deux ailes
> Qui traînent à terre
> Comme des haltères
> Au bout de bretelles,
> L'escargoéland
> Jamais ne se presse :
> Il sait que sans cesse
> L'escargoéland.

Plus fort encore, *Les stations du cri*, qui est un texte assez long, constituant un lipogramme

progressif rétrograde de l'alphabet complet, jusqu'à disparition totale de toutes les lettres, texte

exclusivement pensé en langue française, avec jeux de mots en fin de paragraphe pour justifier à chaque fois la disparition de chaque lettre (« santé ! » pour « sans T », « exit la croix », pour « plus

de x »…) a été traduit en anglais, véritable prouesse, par Chris Clarke.

Aussi, – auparavant (japonais, naturellement), j'en avais discuté avec lui –, j'ai proposé à Chris Clarke le défi suivant : parvenir à traduire un texte que j'écrirais pour l'occasion, un texte qui parlerait de traduction, en le truffant de difficultés de traduction et justifiant l'impossibilité

annoncée de pouvoir me traduire.

> His tail a propeller
> Always flinging his waste
> With the utmost distaste
> This flatulent feller
> The mighty Hipposprey
> Don't dare wander behind
> Unless sure you don't mind
> Beware the Hipposprey

More difficult still was "The Stations of the Cry," which is a fairly long text consisting of a progressive retrograde lipogram of the entire alphabet that ends in the complete disappearance of all its letters, a text conceived of by Olivier exclusively in French, with wordplay at the end of each paragraph to justify the disappearance of each letter ("no longer time for tea" for "no more T," "embalm 'em" for "the end of the M"…), and this I translated into English, which was a veritable feat, according to Olivier Salon.

Then, and he and I discussed this earlier (as opposed to more baronlike, of course), Olivier proposed to me the following challenge: for me to succeed in translating a text that he would write just for the occasion, a text which would speak of translation, and which would be riddled with the many problems of translation, thus justifying the proclaimed impossibility of translating him.

***

Le texte présent est ainsi pensé double, dans les deux langues, et doit être considéré comme une manière de prétérition : j'affirme que ce texte est intraduisible, et je mets Chris Clarke au défi de réussir à traduire le texte que je suis présentement en train d'écrire. Lequel de nous deux sera dans le vrai ? C'est au lecteur de trancher. En tout cas, au lecteur bilingue. Comme le dit Chris lui-même, le texte de départ est le mien, celui d'arrivée est le sien ; mais entre les deux qu'y a-t-il ? C'est cette zone indéfinie que je me propose ici-même d'explorer. Et le texte que j'écris présentement doit être vu comme un aller-retour entre les deux parties, comme une sonate au clair de lune et de l'autre.

Je voulais justement truffer le texte présent de chimères, de coquecigrues (ce fabuleux animal inventé par Rabelais provient probablement de l'accouplement d'un coq avec six grues : ah, là, te

***

And so, the present text has been conceived of doubly, in the two languages, and must be considered a type of apophasis: Olivier averred that this text is untranslatable, and he defied me, Chris Clarke, to succeed in translating the text which he was then in the process of writing. I, in turn, challenge you, my two Outranspian colleagues, Santiago Artozqui and Camille Bloomfield, to translate into French the text I have produced, keeping a subsequent translator in the back of your mind. Who of us will be in the right? It will be up to the reader to decide. In any case, the bilingual reader. As I once told Olivier, the original text is his, the resulting text is mine; and now, your resulting text will be your own... but what lies between them all? It is this undefined zone that he has suggested we explore. And the text I am currently writing must be seen as a round trip between each pair of us, a road you will travel day and night, walking in sunshine and dancing to moonlight, so not a painless road but a beautiful one.

Appropriately, Olivier wanted to fill this particular text with chimeras, with slithy toves (that mythical animal invented by Carroll, which is equal parts lithe and slimy: ah there, you seem

voilà bien perplexe, n'est-ce pas, ami traducteur ? par quel tour de passe-passe, par quel imbroglio, par quelle circonvolution, par quel truchement, par quel artifice digne de la pégomancie vas-tu donc passer ?), d'ichneumons, de billevesées et de phénix.

Je voulais aussi parsemer ce texte de mots rares, mots anciens, mots oubliés, mots scientifiques. Comme si mon texte alambiqué fourmillait de paragraphes corrugateurs, de plissements et de fronces savamment surpiquées au point de bourdon, pour fabriquer des concamérétions spectaculaires.

Il aurait fallu, pour faire bonne mesure, que j'exploitasse plusieurs figures de style, de savantes synecdoques – tout en prenant un verre pour réfléchir à la possible traduction –, des syllepses qui ont l'air bien malicieuses, de fâcheux anacoluthes avec fautes d'accord et pléthore de pléonasmes redondants. Là, tu vois, pauvre traducteur, j'ai dressé un piège terrible car presque invisible : anacoluthe est un mot féminin, auquel j'ai accolé un adjectif masculin, et le diablotin qui

gît en moi a préparé son ressort pour te jaillir à la figure lorsque tu ouvriras la boîte, tant il est vrai que la langue anglaise semble ignorer la différence entre le féminin et le masculin, en tant que genre possible des noms communs. Vois-tu, cela ne me

rather perplexed, aren't you my friend the translator? By what sleight of hand, by what imbroglio, by what circumlocution, by the intervention of what means of expression, by what artifice worthy of pegomancy will you proceed?), with ichneumons, with codswallop and phoenixes.

He also wanted to sprinkle the text with rare words, archaic words, forgotten words, scientific words. As if his alembicated text pullulated with corrugating paragraphs, with plies and frounces eruditely overstitched 'round the bone-lace bobbin so as to craft spectacular concamerations.

For good measure, Olivier felt it necessary to make use of several stylistic devices, which, my fellow translator, thou shalt now need make use of as well, such as sage synecdoches – even as I polish off a glass in hopes that it might provide better reflection for the possible translation –, syllepses who appear malicious and from time to time, and anacolutha upsetting with improper adjective placement and a plethora of redundant pleonasms. What's more, oh wait... no, I can't, I oughtn't, I daren't and I shalln't. 'Tisn't fair, y'all'll hate me, it won't've helped and it musn't've made this any easier. But Imma do it anyway, amn't I? Isn't that just fanfreakingtastic? You betcha! Nuff said. There, you see, poor translator? Just as Olivier laid

gêne en aucune sorte de te montrer du doigt les pièges maléfiques que je dresse à ta science savante, car ce qui me plaît, c'est de te poser des énigmes à visage découvert. Je ne suis pas sournois, crois-le bien : je suis pervers, note bien la différence !

Le pauvre traducteur que voilà ! Lui qui a longtemps fréquenté l'école : n'est-ce pas là, précisément dans les cours d'école qu'il a appris son métier ? Et voilà que je lui flanque comme nouveau piège un mot à la fois épicène et homophonique.

Ah, traducteur ! Contraint de te pencher sur des piles (électriques) de dictionnaires,

a trap for me, I've laid more traps for you, terrible traps, because while these feel quite at home in English, not so much o'er yonder: contractions aren't quite as handy in French, are they? How about double contractions? And triple? And that example of tmesis is a whole nother problem, isn't it? As you can see, the demonling who reposed within Olivier now resides within me, and has wound himself tightly so as to spring out and into your face when you open the box. You see, it in no way bothers me to point out to you the malefic traps that I have laid for your savvy science, much as Olivier pointed out his own to me. What pleases him most is to pose a riddle while looking his victim in the eye. He's not sneaky, believe you me: He is perverse, it's important we both note the difference!

Oh, you poor translators! You've spent such a long time in school. And wasn't it precisely there, in the classroom, that we honed our mutual preference for language games? Yes, that's, like, something like our like like. And there I am tossing you a new trap, a homonym that is preposition, adjective, and noun. Oh, and verb... hope you like it!

Oh, translator! Forced to ponder, weak and weary, hunched over such a lot of dictionaries (stacked high like a pillar of salt),

mes ailes de démon t'empêchent d'officier.

As-tu saisi l'allusion à l'albatros baudelairien ? Que vas-tu faire du dernier alexandrin ? Comment

respecteras-tu l'anacoluthe finale ? Et le jeu de mots que j'invente pour toi à l'instant ? C'est la lutte finale… Cet extrait de l'internationale ne s'accorde-t-il pas admirablement à notre propos polyglotte ? Et ne t'ai-je ainsi pas joué un nouveau tour de Babel ?

as through many constraints and spurious volumes of forgotten lore.

Did you catch the allusion to Poe's raven? When his trochaic octameter you reach, enjoy yourself you will not! How will you manage the hyperbaton I just handed you? And the play on words that I'm coming up with right now? You should take it hyper-quick and start your leg of the relay, from where I've left you, Busted flat in Baton Rouge, all the way to New Orleans, and on to linguistic freedom from there... See, isn't that snippet from Bobby McGee in harmony with our polyglot purposes? After all, you've nothing left to lose! And with that, wouldn't you agree that I've forced your wit to tower higher still should you hope to surpass Babel? If not, Babylon and on we shall.

YELENA MOSKOVICH
I know you know

I was blaming my mother for stuffing so much soul into a lousy body.

+

I was sitting. It was daylight. I was screaming. I couldn't tell which side the pain was on.

+

We order two glasses of red, I, the cheapest, Raphaëlle, finger dosing down the list of wines, "something with a body," she says to the waiter.

+

Just to note, in case it adds up: Money is tight and I live in a studio I had gotten at a bargain for the square meterage, friend-of-a-friend, I pay monthly. Grateful for the small balcony, I overlook the bad plumbing, faint heating, and rotting water deposits in the corners of the ceiling. My unconscious gesture, hands moving like daydreamers, opening and closing drawers, books, the fridge door, as if looking for other rooms.

+

I have refused on many occasions to be frugal in my thirties. I treat myself to spontaneous purchases at the budget home goods store, HEMA, nail polishes to fit my mood (2,50 euros), an occasional scented candle (3,50 euros), and in dire acts of kindness, a fresh, new towel (7,50 euros). I refill my perfume bottle with water, and spray myself with a diluted essence (originally 98 euros). Still, *chez moi*, the shower drain smells of warm cabbage. The smell of warm cabbage embarrasses me. I mean, the solace and the burden of my mother's body heat.

+

Giving into an impulse for new bedding was no small thing. The full rose-coloured linen set (pillow cases, sheets, duvet-cover) was 79,99 euros (on sale), and though I couldn't afford it, I opened my wallet as if birds could fly out, bagged it, and came home, gloating with nerves. I took my clothes off and fell into my new rose-coloured linen, stomach first, rubbing my contours into the cotton planes as if redrawing my skin, shoulders, ass, and so on.

+

"I'd rather just sit on the couch with the cat than have sex," Raphaëlle pronounces. She sits up slightly and adjusts her jeans, than sits back down, a habit of hers I know well, since she doesn't like the jean button pressing into her scar.

+

It's true that Raphaëlle stays in mostly, with her boyfriend and her aging cat. Our friendship is long-standing, but in the last years, maintained increasingly through Facebook messenger exchanges, our complicity shortcut into cat stickers, our shame into shy monkey emojis, and our sense of powerlessness into gifs of stuck kittens. I had other friends and occasional girlfriends and she had her boyfriend and her cat. I had gotten used to her canceled plans, and she, to the hyper-activity of my lonely heart. Both of us, growing older like stone faces spitting out our youth.

+

Also, in case it adds up, I don't know why she picked a café neither in her neighbourhood nor mine, but rather smack dab in front of the Notre Dame cathedral, its retro brown awning sagging with rain-water. The terrace heaters were on, and we sat down shivering, trying to recognize each other, me with my pushy smile, her, with her glum hauteur. Our legs crossed in the same direction, her tawny hair pulled over her left shoulder, eyes made-up with shimmering taupe, and lips dabbed a dark brick colour to match her russet wool coat.

+

We were laughing about darker and heavier subjects when the second glass came and went. Even the waiter seemed sloppy, glass-rings of spilled red wine on the cold counter-top. I can't remember exactly when the Russian woman interrupted Raphaëlle and I, but it was after Raphaëlle had divulged a memory like a hair-clump. The story she was telling seemed so pivotal to her personage, I wondered how it was that we had known each other all these years, and she had never mentioned it.

+

She was four years old, in day-care, *it was a gloomy day*, Raphaëlle is insisting, *like today*. The sun had never come out. Little Raphaëlle had a yellow coloured pencil in her hand. She hiked up her ruffle-trimmed dress and pulled down the leggings she had underneath. Then, pulling her underwear to the side, Little Raphaëlle began to slide the yellow coloured pencil inside herself, as deep as it would go. Before the day-care teacher could intervene, awkwardly pulling her little legs apart, trying to fish the pencil out, Raphaëlle had stuck two more up there, a green one and a brown one. The rest happened so quickly, it felt almost as if she had chosen it. By the afternoon, little Raphaëlle was in the hospital with a frizzy-haired woman who must have been a civil servant appointed for her best interest, and a gynaecologist was telling her that she would feel something strange down-there and that it was okay. When the four-year-old asked for her mom, the doctor explained that she could not be there right now, but that her grandma was on her way. Raphaëlle's grandmother, a fast-paced skeleton, marched into the hospital with her fur-trimmed coat and her gray chignon, and upon entering the room, began explaining to the doctor about the unfit mother who was her *triste* daughter. She spotted Raphaëlle laid out on the examination table, rushed to her and put her bony hands with all her cold rings upon Raphaëlle's hot face, snapping her head back at the doctor, glaring with her feral pupils, and yelling, "She must have hurt her to hurt *me*." All the while Raphaëlle's mom was taken to the police station, where she was asked a series of questions, including about the child's father, who was not present, her mother explained, because he was a busy man, too busy being a piece of shit, officer. Her mother had always been cactus tongued when cornered, like her own mother, the fur-coat with an unending desert. It was finally sorted out that Raphaëlle's pencil stunt was not a sign of abuse within the home, the absent father and present mother exonerated as non-molesters, but a misunderstanding of a little girl's artistic expression. "I could have told them myself, if they'd asked me directly! Hadn't seen my Dad since I was two, and my mom was too lazy to give me a hug," Raphaëlle took a sip of her wine, "let alone fondle me!" *Lazy* was a word Raphaëlle used for depression, another trait she shared with her mother. "I mean, I think I would've been overjoyed, really, I would've been on cloud-nine if my mom had put in the time and effort to molest me!"

+

"…And when they finally did ask me why it was that I had stuck those coloured pencils into my four-year-old-cunt, I told them I had wanted draw a sun there. Cause it was too dark. And a tree too, so I could climb up to my heart."

+

Goddamn the smell of warm cabbage. Raphaëlle is laughing with her ashen voice. It's flaking. It's dandruff on my anger. Four, five, six, and so on. Me, in the Soviet Union. I spent those years waiting for instructions. And still to this day, all-grown and Western, I mistake guidelines for love.

When the Russian woman came up to us, it was on my side, just over my shoulder. I could feel her Russianness approaching. Raphaëlle had stopped talking and the woman touched my shoulder and asked in a splintered English where the fountain was.

+

Pozhalusta, Please, she said, switching over to Russian with me as if she knew.

+

I'm tilting my head up towards her, a Soviet perspective of motherhood, though she is my age, dark hair like me, long nose, serious brow, but her face is a blur or else my eyes are a blur or maybe it's my memory.

+

Gdye fontan? She asks me bluntly.

+

She pushes her phone towards my face, Google maps on the screen, as her fingertip smudges around the whole neighbourhood, *gdye ohn?* Where is it?

+

That's right. I do remember that right before the Russian woman interrupted us, Raphaëlle and I had a lull in the conversation where both our eyes drifted past each other, hers to the spires upon the gothic cathedral behind me, and mine, along the gutter bars at the curb. Then she said that in life, she doesn't like to hold a grudge, she has forgiven all her friends and lovers and family who have done her wrong, even that ex who beat her for the last year of their relationship (her words), but there was one person she would never forgive. Josephine. Her oldest friend, a *camarade de classe* in that preschool where she tried to draw inside herself like the cave of Lascaux. They had lost touch for years then re-found each other in their early twenties and lived their party-girl years as roommates, until one thing led to another and Raphaëlle's late-term abortion left her with a scar on her belly and Josephine, sleeping with the baby's father behind her back. "It's not that I want revenge." Raphaëlle is assuring me. "I heard Josephine's father passed away last autumn." Her eyes are grazing the rim of her glass, trying to make music. "I'd like to dig up her father's grave and throw his cadaver into her bed while she's sleeping," she says without tone or heart.

+

"Do you mean the fountain near the Saint Michel metro?" I remember Raphaëlle trying to ask the Russian woman. *Nye etot*! She jerked her phone away from us. Not that one. "But there is no fountain right here," I was explaining. *Da, yest,* yes there is, she insisted. Look, I was pointing, This is a café. There's the Seine, There's Notre Dame. I have cigarettes, if you—*NYE*T! The woman slammed our tabletop with her open palm and just like that, I was afraid. *GDYE FONTAN?* The woman shouted. My glass of wine tipped off the table and shattered at my feet. My chin was down, *Nyetu fontana*, I mumbled. There is no fountain. *YEST*! There is! Her fingers were gripping her phone so hard, I thought Google maps would burst into my face. I lowered my glance, across the table, looking for Raphaëlle. Just like that, she wasn't there anymore. Just the empty chair. I don't know why, it didn't surprise me. Just the screaming from above. *GDE GDE GDE*. Just my knuckles trembling at my brow. WHERE. Just covering my face. Just the blame. Just the blot. Just the lack of surprise. Right then. She slammed the phone she was gripping against my skull. The screen, the streets. Cracked on my forehead. Cuts against my scalp. It stung all over. My crown, my ear. And her voice, so close to me, dripping, from beneath my skin, her voice, bleeding down my face, *I know you know, I know you know.*

CAMILLE BLOOMFIELD

Image Credit: Delphine Presles

Poems for Brexitees

Camille Bloomfield

to my parents,
Keith and Geneviève Charbonneau-Bloomfield

Year 2022 : « Hard Brexit » has won and it has become very difficult to circulate between France and Great Britain. Times are rough for the Franco-British nationals, for the Paris-London commuters, for the Brits of France and the French of Britain, for all of those who have been brexited. They now wander, nostalgic, stuck between their two cultures in one of their two countries.

To support them in these times of adversity, inspired by my Outranspo fellows, I composed a series of poems especially for them :
- a few lazy beginner's poems – special translations of classics from both sides of the Channel for those who want to capture the essence of a language & practice their accent without having to learn any actual word,
- a reassuring poem in French, for English-speakers who think they don't understand French
- a embracing poem and its translation in English, for those who like it when two (or more !) languages meet in one single word
- an Entente cordiale poem, for those who do not want to have to chose between French and English and favor transparency & neutrality
- a snob poem, for bilingual readers only, who are able to perceive the strangeness of linguistic loans & inventions

Tick tock tick tock riiiiiing
Lazy beginner's poems

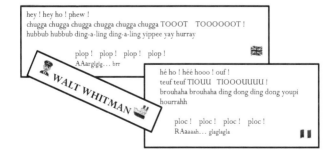

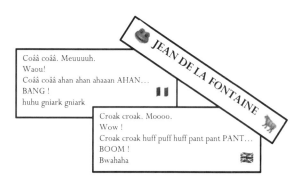

Coââ coââ. Meuuuuh.
Waou!
Coââ coââ ahan ahan ahaaan AHAN…
BANG !
huhu gniark gniark

Croak croak. Moooo.
Wow !
Croak croak huff puff huff pant pant PANT…
BOOM !
Bwahaha

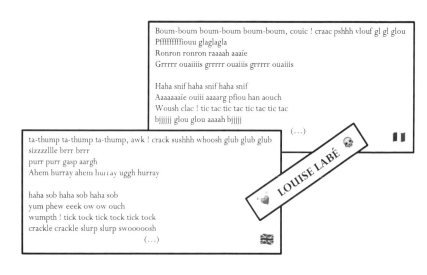

Boum-boum boum-boum boum-boum, couic ! craac pshhh vlouf gl gl glou
Pffffffffiouu glaglagla
Ronron ronron raaaah aaaïe
Grrrrr ouaiiis grrrrr ouaiiis grrrrr ouaiiis

Haha snif haha snif haha snif
Aaaaaaaïe ouiii aaaarg pfiou han aouch
Woush clac ! tic tac tic tac tic tac tic tac
bjjjjjj glou glou aaaah bjjjjj
(…)

ta-thump ta-thump ta-thump, awk ! crack sushhh whoosh glub glub glub
sizzzzlllle brrr brrr
purr purr gasp aargh
Ahem hurray ahem hurray uggh hurray

haha sob haha sob haha sob
yum phew eeek ow ow ouch
wumpth ! tick tock tick tock tick tock
crackle crackle slurp slurp swooooosh
(…)

A Brexitee's day
Reassuring poem (*en français*)

8 :00 : Earl grey, croissant,
Marmite-baguette.

8 :45 : chauffeur :)
9 :00 : en route !

9 :30 : co-working : Start up-Nation.
Mail.
Meetings.
Pitch projet leadership.
Conf-call business plan, paper-board disruptif, workshop post-it, app, aaapp, aaaaaaaaaAAPP

12 :30 Prêt-à-manger.
Sandwich & Coca Zero.
Menu de luxe… :/

14 :10 : Boutique prêt-à-porter/couture.
Lingerie chic.
Culotte orange & blazer pastel
Style Michelle Obama.
Nb. budget max 300 eu !!!

18 :00 Toilette express

19 :00 : rendez-vous, restaurant The Frexit.
Apéritif avec M. + fiancé R. + fiancée C. (!! ménage à trois !!)
C. : brunette, petite, cute. Un je-ne-sais-quoi de déjà-vu.
R. : sihouette XXL, eau de Cologne, tatoué.

Atmosphère pique-nique.
Menu à la carte, chef cool… Bon appétit !

20 :00 : Hors d'oeuvre
+ Soupe / Omelette
+ salade vinaigrette
+ Bordeaux / Café / Whisky

23 : 00 : soirée Sarah
look bourgeois, design cosy
artistes avant-garde = clichééé
Musique funk, swing, soul – répertoire vintage
vibes +++
Alcool (vodka russe !)
Target : S.
1 rock /1 salsa /1 slow → 1 smack… yes !
Souvenirs sexy… Go ? Go !

« - Voulez-vous coucher avec moi ?
- … Comme ci, comme ça.

- 🌀

- Lol. Ok, hm… ciao, bye ! »

Étonnante Athena
Poème embrassant *(original version)*

Alors que les **auto***cars* venus de tout le pays
vomissent leurs vagues de voyageurs sur l'avenue,
que ceux-ci **four**mi*llant* se répandent sur le port,
là où musiques *tear*-**larmes**,
fumets d'**auberge**-*inn* et de poisson grillé
s'échappent des gargotes traditionnelles,
je regarde étonnée les marins *att***inant**
leur navire ;
        ils se préparent sans sourire
à l'absence des putes,
aux horizons houleux
de capitaines *born*-**nés**.

Soudain la vois-*see*, elle se dresse parmi eux
c'est l'**A**t**he**n**a** moderne,
déesse des *barbar*es
au sein nu tatoué de slogans peu amènes
                      en lettres majuscules.
Shorty *sílly***conne** et **perd**-*loose* au collier,
en lieu et place de lance, son poing serré, levé.

Elle est le verbe haut et la fièvre *Ebb***ola**
la hantise des Weinstein et des Coca-Cola
Dans son sillage ce n'est que
gestes affolés malaises **va***go* cris d'orfraie
sur son passage
les hommes serrent les jambes,
détournent les yeux
et hémorragent honteux
                        devant sa nudité :
ils pleurent déjà de se savoir *com*m*and***é**s
vaincus qu'ils sont déjà,
à la mer*sea* d'**A**t**he**n**a**.

Astonishing Athena
Embracing poem (*a literal translation*)

As the buses coming from all over the country
vomit their waves of travellers onto the avenue,
their swarm spreading out on the port,
where tear-jerker music,
scents of aubergine and grilled fish
escape from traditional taverns,
surprised I watch the sailors place their ship
on keelblocks ;
                without a smile they are preparing themselves
for the absence of whores,
for stormy horizons
and stubborn captains.

Suddenly here she is, she rises amongst them
modern Athena
goddess of the Barbarians :
on her naked breast are tattooed unfriendly slogans
                              in capital letters.
Silicon mini-shorts, beads on her necklace,
instead of a spear, her fist, raised, clenched.

She is the soaring verb and the Ebola fever
the dread of the Weinsteins and the Coca-Colas
in its wake it's all
panicked gestures, fainting attacks, screams of bloody murder
as she passes by
men close their legs,
look away
and haemorrhage ashamed
                    before her nudity :
they cry, conscious of being under orders
defeated as they already are
at Athena's mercy.

RIP MOTIVATION
Entente cordiale poem

Pain ? bizarre.
Chat ? impatient.
Bras sale ? impossible.
Main sale ? banal.

MINCE EMOTION
SINGE SENSATION
POUR SATISFACTION...
RIP MOTIVATION.

A sympathetic day
Snob poem

Hard morning.
No hot water.
No make up.
Hair looking awful.
I should never pay so much for such an old-fashioned brushing.
Now I'm standing anxious in front of my unlit dressing…
Why should I change that bulb anyway ?
And who cares if I don't ?

Next step. Clothes.
What best matches my mood today ?
Pink pull-over, white skirt, glitter string
and the usual pair of wedge heels baskets
that make me look grander ?
Or a gender bender black smoking with a funky yellow tie ?
Oh wait, no, I forgot to pick these up from the pressing.
Obviously.
Too bad for my last-minute relooking.
I'll go for the hot tenniswoman style.
I can always pretend I'm about to do a running
or even a footing
in the park
with my cute little dog.
Act like I'm sporty.
Nobody will ever believe me but hey,
still worth trying.

OK. Now.
One thing after the other.
Get out of the flat.
Find car at the parking.
Where the hell did I leave it last night ?
There's still so much booze in my brain.
I think I did a bad trip. Again.
Hope no one remembers.
Keep on going.
You can do it.
Order a builder's tea at your usual drive-in.
Ask for the addition.
Complain 'cause the credit card machine doesn't work.
Try paying by check. Computer says no.
Shout at the useless and hairy barman that he's useless and hairy.
Leave without my tea.
Injure him once you're windows are closed.
He abuses, after all.
Ok, I could've paid in liquid.
I had some in my wallet.
I could've proposed at least.
Can't be bothered.

The thing is
when your actual life consists in

translating baby-foot user's manuals
for low-cost French companies,
or doing play-back on crappy clips
for second range reality-tv,
when your week is a permanent zapping
between your various day-jobs
and when you know that class affair
will never be for you
you'll always have to demand favors
and people will always say no
'cause no one wants to be comprehensive
towards people like you,
you,
well,
me.
It's definitely not my day of chance.
I'd better get back to bed and achieve my book.
That only never deceives me.

STEWART HOME
Paris By Numbers AKA I Am A Punk Rock Cliche

I don't understand your plea to live – "one wonders if this 'thinking' woman's punk act were familiar with Lettrist cinema or the Zanziba Group, although their focus is clearly on more commercial movies." There's a bottle in the corner – "it's French wine but if it was whiskey it would probably be Johnny Walker or Jack Daniels; do punk rockers drink Springbank and Laphroaig?" Inventer la liberté. I look so debonaire – "irony, the band's image in based in part on the film *A Clockwork Orange.*" Young Parisians are so French – "oxymoron." Here I am with my child on the Eiffel tower – "tourist cliché." A secret history of a time to come – "there's no future for *no future.*" Walking towards the boulevard. Well if you've been to cities but you've had enough. Sentimental through the night – "it's enough to make you fall asleep." The first days of winter – "not to mention the first and last days of spring, summer and fall." I'm on the top, with the job. She makes me so unsure of myself. Take me to Paris.

Or the guy's wish to take or give – "homosociality is not necessarily an attack on patriarchy". That's where I'm gonna stay. Fichés traqués matraqués. I haven't got a care in this world, this crazy world – "a softening of the 'I don't care' proclamation so prominent in seventies punk rock." They love Patti Smith – "but do they love Robert Mapplethorpe?" Looking down. The free explosion, everyone must search. She's studied it all before. Have you been to Paris, France? – "A question seemingly aimed at Americans." Sharing secret candlelight. I can't hold onto. Jumping to my death – "can suicide ever be romantic?" Standing there but never talking sense. Give me wine, give me company, give me leisure – "the communist project of disalienation will end all such canalised divisions."

However as backing away. Just me and my bottle of French wine. Face aux nervis camoufles. And I act oh so suave – "any old irony?" Young Parisians are so French – "since some embrace other national identities such as being Algerian, and others reject all forms of national identity, are they necessarily French?" When the light disappears – "the desperate will steal almost anything, including the fittings from your apartment." For what he loves and for what attracts him – "desire is productive but it can also be repressive." She buys herself a seat – "a toilet seat?" And if you doubt that Paris was made for love, give Paris one more chance. We're away. All the days. It's Paris the Tower Eiffel - "tourist cliché." Just a visitor you see – *"tourism, human circulation considered as consumption is fundamentally nothing more than the leisure of going to see what has become banal."* Let me brush your hair – "or should we consider the possibility of shaving the pubes?"

He fell and lay dead amongst the firework display. We're gonna drink the night away. Solides gardiens de l'appris. Sophisticated, boy I've got it all, I'm a star – "some may wonder which star, Alpha Centauri A, B or C, or a more distant heavenly body?" Paris is a frozen town – "we are bored in the city, *there is no longer any Temple of the Sun.*" At the Champs Elysee - "tourist cliché." So I took Eric, Mr. Satie to an Algerian Rai Club – "are we supposed to view Satie as a precursor to punk rock minimalism?" And sits on the floor - *"Chairs Missing?"* The home of Piaf and Chevalier – "Le Piaf was a French automobile of the 1950s, while a Chevalier is a rank in certain orders of knighthood." Every day. Of my youth. The sexiest building left. So much wanting to be seen. Let me hold you for a little while – "be my prisoner?"

It's not quite the way to say your goodbyes. Nobody comes, nobody knocks on the door. Payes armés pour nous tuer. Dance the night away - "super cliché." I want to go to Paris with you – "what about Alytus or Valencia?" Now she turns her face to the camera. Losing James Bond in Pigalle – "combined spy fiction and tourist cliché." Taking in a picture show – "the 'art' of seduction." Must have done something right to get passion this way – "if passion ends in fashion then Marine Le Pen is the best dressed man in town." Laughing, joking just sustains. All the graces of love.

I've been waiting here for far too long – "there is no beginning, there is no end, it goes on forever..." She'd open up the door and vaguely carry us away. Nothing to measure – "off-the-peg lyrics, clichés work!"

It's not quite the way to behave – "decorum is overrated." My friends are far away. Paris maquis quotidian. Down in gay Paris – "super cliché." Just to see what the French boys do – girl tomorrow, boy today! A photograph – "*Camera Lucida* is an inquiry into the meaning of photography and simultaneously a eulogy to the dead mother of its author Roland Barthes." Was the best night I ever had – "hierarchical thought is evident here." She doesn't know where to go. If you don't think Paris was made for love, give Paris one more chance. Situation quite insane – "madness is the only sane response to the insanity of capitalist society." Are over now. I look around for something strong – "personally I'd go for a gorilla in an old dark house." It's the customary thing to say or do. No one to please.

Secured you a concrete grave. If the telephone don't start ringing. Un jeu truqué où tu perds. Dance the night away – "return of the super cliché." Why don't you come to Paris with me? And the river is a diamond snake – *"as beautiful as the chance encounter of an umbrella and a sewing machine on an operating table."* La la la la, c'est nul. Is it a film or is it real? Well now I'm calling it arrogant, calling it cruel, give Paris one more chance. Flowing wine – *"it's a wonder I don't fall, my mind's not on my work at all."* For you. My heart beats on and on – "and it won't be transplanted till the break of dawn." To a disappointed proud man in his grief – "the price paid for failing to release his inner woman." No one to see – *"this is the night in which all cows are black."*

Beneath the motorway – "the underpass." It's gonna be a bad bad day – "bad is merely the antithesis of good and the notion of hierarchy is required to mediate between them." Terrerur meurtre ā chaque instant. On the Champs-Elysees – "return of the tourist cliché." And see the young Parisians. Around her head – "if it's a bandage then this is the return of the mummy, no longer maiden not yet crone…" She went into the movie – *"La Grande Illusion?"* And also trop civilisé et mon dieu, c'est trop cool. Quite sublime – "without any philosophical enquiry." For you. And suddenly I can't think clear – "high on booze and narcissism." And on Fridays she'd be there. Run naked through the street – "rock & roll, dope and touring the world in a transit van."

Gold scissors cut the ribbon and set them loose – "a procession of simulacra." Ooh la la la, ooh la lay –"for 14 years from 1970 the BBC screened Play For Today." Drôle d'etat assassin. Dance the night away – "time to collect your coats and go home." Young Parisians are so French. I can't see it anymore – "those who stare at the sun go blind." La la la la, on m'l'a fait plus. She's been there ever since – "quiet days in Puteaux?" Give Paris one more chance. Not so far for me to say. And I will never bear my skin for you – "fuck patriarchy, get nude for communism!" Getting close I sit close to you –"slipshod repetition." And on Wednesday not at all. And drink Champagne – "the first sip tastes like shit and the next even worse…"

On the opening days the vibrations will shake your bones – "le weekend starts here." There's a party in Paris today. Fragilite liberté. Down in gay Paris – "some prefer grey London, others greyer Glasgow." They sit on the Metro – *"going down on the underground."* Nobody's knocking on my door. Non, non, non moi j'aime personne. She walked out to the lobby – "on her hands?" But if you don't think Paris was made for love, maybe your heart needs a telegram from up above. I could take you there today – "on the Eurostar or by private plane?" And feel you once more. Suddenly I fear and fear – "fear is a powerful emotion but its invocation here is blatantly rhetorical." Just casually appearing from the clock across the hall. And make you love me even more than you do – "coercion is abuse."

I suppose that's the disadvantage. I turn on the radio – "by caressing the dials and smothering it with kisses?" Révolution Résistance. Dance the night away – "*Adieu la vie, adieu l'amour (Kiss Tomorrow Goodbye).*" Young Parisians are so French – "down with immutable identities!" And we dream that we fall with a parachute – "don't fall, fly!" Stripping on the catwalks of those tiny dimly lit clubs. For a box of Junior Mints – "*Get Stupid

Fresh Part 2." If you don't think Paris was made for love, well give Paris one more chance. Let's tango in Paris – "Brando, Bertolucci and butter equal rape." In beauty's remorse – "no regrets." I feel sexy up so high – "distance is relational and not rational." You're a ghost la la la – "seduction is destiny." Who have we become?

Of not speaking a second language – *"wine will make you a linguist, it will teach you Greek in two hours."* But I don't like what they play – "too many minor chords?" Paris maquis quotidian. Make it sleazy – *"live fast, die young and have a good looking corpse."* Not like me and you – *"Saturday Night and Sunday Morning (Millions Like Us)."* Like angles do. Girls who turn from time to time into animals – "let's trash the old patriarchal myth of beauty and the beast." She never looks beyond the mirror – "in punk rock bricolage everything is pure surface." Well now there's some things I don't like and some things I do, but give Paris one more chance. You might find yourself with me – *"hell is other people."* No more hope only time and what's left – "duration is ineffable." Feel my treasure chest. You're a ghost. Something better, something heavy – "a 32kg kettlebell?"

A second language – "Spanish and Cantonese." So I put a record on the stereo. La ville zombie régulee. I am a mystery – "more like history." I want to go to Paris with you. We look at the world through the eyes of birds – "gender is a cultural construct." And then back into animal girls – "learn to speak the language of the birds."

Or the image that appears – "five parts bullshit to one part hesitation." I can see why Paris would be ugly for you but give Paris one more chance. Share your glass of vanity – *"that which appears is good, that which is good appears."* Of the fountains. Let's have sex before I die – "only if there is consent." I'm in the church and I've come to claim you with my iron drum la la la la la la – *"La Rose de Fer (1973)."* Something together - "the switch to nothing is becoming...."

A second language – "English as a second language." Just to pass this night away – "reclaim the night." Musés blindés de l'appris. Not what I seem to be, oh no – *"I am nothing therefore I must become everything."* Just to see what the French boys do. Feather words. Drinking at the well of their true desires – *"I drink therefore I am!"* Well, I just watch the world go by – "voyeurism by any other name would be as kinky." The home of Piaf and Trenet too must have done something right – "I'd rather hear *Quelle crise, Baby*, even if Starshooter were from Lyon." We're away. I have nothing. It will be my sexual best. The continent's just fallen in disgrace – "you've just fallen flat on your face." Holding all your hands - *"Octopussy."*

A second language. Just to pass this night away – "Henri Bergson saw repetition as the basis of all humour." La ville resiste terroriste. It's so Parisian – "Kierkegaard believed the British did boredom best." Why don't you come to Paris with me? I can't feel it anymore – "Bertrand Russell's table?" Drinking at the well of their true desires – "crossed wires." And try to get her attention – "Viennese sausages." Must have something for you. Every day. And waiting for me. I'm waiting here to be saved – "you may have to settle for being recycled." William Rogers put it in its place. So lucky and unlucky – "barely an oxymoron."

A second language – "Tagalog?" It's twelve'o'clock, I can see them now – "sick of perception." Assassine l'état dans la poche. I am a masquerade – *"Halloween Parade?"* And see the young Parisians. Nobody's knocking on my door. Drinking at the well of their true desires – "those who deal in sexual abuse are deceitful above all things." Scream at her, and I yell and scream at her – "Edvard Munch." If you don't think Paris was made for love, give Paris one more chance. Not so far for me to say. All the white that's inside – "white radiant tranquillity, red blazing energy, black maturity, the three colours of matriarchy." By someone strong and someone brave. Blood and tears from old Japan – "Orientalism has a long history." We'll always remember – "until we forget."

Bad reception results in blurred perception – "overthrow all hierarchy." They're dancing the night away – *"They Shoot Horses Don't They?"* Je te juge l'état contre moi. Just a man-parade – "a cliché, wrapped in a death culture, inside the patriarchy." Alors et maintenant. Drinking at the well of their true desires

– "if I am, death is not, if death is, I am not." And I scream, ice cream, I scream! Now hear the boys singing Bee Gees songs under the skies, give Paris one more chance - *"Spicks and Specks* or *To Love Somebody?"* I could take you there today. In the morning mist - *"your imagination is worth more than you imagine."* What I feel my legs grow weak. Caravans and lots of jam and maids of honour – "let them dream of beefcake." No one to please – "not even yourself?"

A second language. Little Jimmy's dressed as Fred Astaire – *"I'll be your clown or your puppet or your April Fool."* Fasciste! So I dance, I dance with you – *"Me And You Doin' The Boogaloo."* I want to go to Paris with you – "and Bolbaite and Bolinas too." We land in a street where poets live – "revolution is poetry." Drinking at the well of their true desires – "truth is a fiction." I scream Merry Eiffel Tower High! And on the steps of Montmartre they harmonise, give Paris one more chance. Let's tango in Paris. In the crystal air – *"the social void is scattered with interstitial objects and crystalline clusters which spin around and coalesce in a cerebral chiaroscuro."* And my voice it starts to squeak – "noteworthy aspects of Squeak include a simple yet efficient incremental garbage collector for 32-bit direct pointers." Singing crying singing tediously. *Take Me To Paradise.*

AMALIE BRANDT

when you're crying every night because of some character that doesn't even exist. when it is a cheap and sloppy narrative trope. when victims get their mind wiped. when freshly mind-changed characters convinced they live in a certain place go there only to find an empty lot. when later in the story they go to a party at a friend's house where the "wife" is pulled into a pantry and vigorously fucked by someone assumed to be the "husband." when it turns out it wasn't. when you make a new character two paragraphs later that occupies the space of the previous one. when you're trying to pitch it to some capitalist fucklord. when they're trying to fight the change. when it is no longer important to them as they embrace their new identity. when essentially it is murder. when you kill someone to build a new person out of his or her corpse. when at least they took the bodies of people who were already dead. when characters that you recognise pretend they are not who they are. when it involves the unwilling theft of someone's body. when you feel sorry for the original owner of the body. when you hope she comes back and takes control. when he is just a voice inside Janice's head now. when the murderer never existed in the first place but Jill is still not alive. when there was an error but they can't change him back. when she's now happy to continue as Gus. when you don't know whether or not they are in their "real" bodies. when people take advantage of it to become who they want. when lyrics in a story doesn't work even if the characters are listening to the song. when characters can't forget about their own normal reality either. when the protagonist overcomes a smoking habit. when they replace you with a changed version of yourself. when even the new personality hates the guy. when a character acquires a different name for no apparent reason. when she seems to be two different persons in each of the stories. when it is in someones interest to kill off a character. when corruption and clothes alter the person. when ideally he wakes up transformed into a copy of Veronica. when it is confusing to have the identity jump around. when part of the dialogue seems to be coming out of the wrong person. when the alter ego voice appears speaks and then goes away. when you find out about the other person through her own perspective instead of by the third person. when he looks at Bobby and sees himself. when they continue playing cards under the circumstances. when it is unbelievable that the mom gets arrested. when the baby is talking like an adult. when you've lost track of the characters and who they are. when nobody does anything and things just happens to them. when the new April is a wife but is also a girlfriend of the former Lucinda and is running away. when they exist as nothing more than names. when she is not really dead but completely changed. when the people appearing at the end laugh at the main character.

IAN MONK
9 nick-fucks in Paris's anatomical extent
By Houssine Bouchama
(utterly mistranslated by Ian Monk)

Self-farming and scoffing: the ultimate coms

The earth splits into two headers: one having the reflection that nick-fucks are just a liaison with industrial sausages, in a northern French town while over-living, and another with a sexual prison sentence from scoffing and slurping in utter openness while breast-feeding a ghost.By prising apart an apprentice, you have flopped out in the latter rubric. Come well. And kudos. Right on, you'll be letting yourself loose from the mid-year bowling surface of the Buttes-Chaumont, where no later than the day before you were getting cirrhosis from a not very enthusiastic pinkie, while examining a nearby, large, bodily protuberance tickling your salami. Right on, you can polish yourself in corporations, groggy on hateful days, about your sabbath nick-fuck when you flung yourself onto some equipment for an advanced technique in an abundant bush, with a lighter and housed piss-heads or else a carved mammoth in the countryside of the Reigning Pinwheel.

It remains to say: you will have pierced the fringe for a yummy bolus of cool techniques in the Essonne, in Seine-Saint-Denis, in Yvelines or else Val-de-Marne, in the kernel of implausible pollocks where advanced techniques and heirlooms share rooms quite crudely. It remains to say: your womb will be solid and the ghost will be brisk. Short-lived, you'll still be upgraded.

Lovely leaking – Domaine de Chamarande

Drafts lead to a monastic controversy when it comes to the Domaine de Chamarande. The vineyard of the Essonne and its glamorous fleet, roosting on the verge of timber and of a faint settlement bound to the RER C line, are a non-platonic site for scoffing, with a little technique, a dry sausage on a patchy slick. From the bowling surface for the blind, advance technical exposures (here with a 17th-century vineyard); in this place, farming rhymes with residential techniques and, with foxy delight, we flutter from one erection to the next, before tramping amidst charities, slumping on weed, and letting ourselves drip along the field's watery plain, on some bark which has been bent completely gratuitously.

Below the pinwheel – Château de Versailles

It's hard to scamper into a corner for weed, farming or a French inheritance without passing by a hut in Versailles. If you lack the spunk to stuff yourself while visiting the vineyard, you can still get a bolus of techniques and tales from the playpen, pegged as it is with neo-normal and advanced carvings, like panellists conversing with pollocks. When it comes to getting consolation, the yards contain several rooms devoted to nick-fucks. What else could the nation request?

Whipped wind – Galleria Continua

The Galleria Continua likes to behold stuff in droves. This ancient mill measuring 10,000m² is a blatant agitation in the Seine-et-Marne: it is where the booted Mario Cristiani, Lorenzo Fiaschi and Maurizio Rigillo, who already had their knobs out in two porches in San Gimignano and Beijing, steadied their trunks in 2007. Working mammoths and showy joints to get high give the splits to this mighty plot of rattles, glue and foliage. A tasty guise for dipping your potato into the lotion of advanced techniques.

On the bowling surfaces of the FRAC – Parc culturel de Rentilly

Pegged to the FRAC Ile-de-France since the egos of a final November, the Rentilly vineyard, newly translated into an advanced technique campus, constantly earmarks glamorous astonishments, within buttocks and their glimmering features, as pictured by Xavier Veilhan. This advanced track should be supplemented by a nick-fuck in the yard, far away from pop and pavements.

In the carving grove – Cité de la céramique

Carvings, chattels and assorted potted purposes illegally occupy these houses all year. An impeccable guise for a nick-fuck with a small chick, uneventfully, on some carved umber. A little indulgence, though! Because positions are precious. This graphic Cité has just one hammered shoe in its yards and only a few shoals as a starter...

The obscurantist hour – Abbaye de Maubuisson

Here, middle-age's penis is still with it. As an antique monkish shack, Maubuisson has been like a downtown especially sheltering advanced techniques since 2000. But with reduced steps: exposures, flaunted across the entire playpen, and coming between the berms of the abbey's shed, play on each other with spunk and inventiveness. This is a non-platonic launching-site for slaking technical cravings, beneath a design of warhead canopies and recently stained glasses, before steadying your shopping cart of cash amidst a 10,000-hectare yard. Nicely tantalizing, natch.

On the verge of tears – CNEAI

Roosted on this inklings' isle, at the core of really ritzy, really idiosyncratic occidental commuters, the Centre National Edition d'Art et Images of Chatou tells tales amid the sunniest unknown farming flying objects in Paris's anatomical extent. Thanks to its sheer labia for advanced techniques, it beds piss-heads in an abode above a fluttering company (with a lighter lashed onto the foot of its space) and embraces exposures all year long. It's enough to rinse your eyes and be openly tantalizing before delving into the ways that so dazzled Renoir and his lady friends. A port area of foliage and farming, quintessential for revelling in your cured pork and grease, trimmed by the Seine.

In an obsessed density – Le Cyclop

Do you cherish shooting the rich, freakish pollocks, and unearthly techniques that leak out from dull wrecks so as to shove themselves into a complete character? Then this jauntiness is being performed for you. Just think about a few pinwheel spokes, amid shafts, striking through a deciduous surround, with abruptly a 23-metre high frameless noodle, made up of a motley blending of 300 tonnes of rattles and variegated clockwork. This is the "Cyclop" by Jean Tinguely and Niki de Saint Phalle, a mega, fruity job, haphazard, unprompted and multi-family, whose unparalleled stare shivers the timbers of Milly-la-Forêt. Weaponize yourself with a fine nick-fuck shopping-cart, then furrow its woody routes to localize a non-platonic glade.

With a numerical demeanour – Château Ephémère

Just half a twinkle from Paris by RER, this vineyard of fashionable weather, unveiled in June 2015, buoyantly vindicates bending. As navigated by the audible and numerical Fabrique, this burying ground gives us the third degree, and 2,000m^2 of exposures, piss-head housing, scored bedsits, bees, consultations, fabulous labia, etc. The kingpin William Kissam's ancient purview thus makes us come again, live, after a dozen years running between excesses and recovery, under the moral constraint of novel electronic components and numerical, audible techniques. And vibrating all around this palate of dots, there is a far-reaching playpen of 6,000m^2... Just right to nick-fuck with a numerical demeanour. If you have misplaced your shopping-cart's spread, there will be no compulsion to upend Paris, given that a decked canteen has just unlocked its lifts.

ANDREW GALLIX
Macron Death Party

'Once upon a time…'

She looked up from the big picture book.

'Lie down now, there's a good boy, or I shan't read you a bedtime story.'

Her voice was stern but soothing. Soon it would speak from some secret wound, secreting senseless squander. Tales of strange voyages to enigmatic climes would pour forth; unmoored, rudderless. Suddenly he felt himself all at sea: drowning in the wide inky-black yonder, dissolving like sugar in absinthe. Giant crabs threw him sidelong glances. Tentacles coiled, vine-like, around his legs and testicles. Mermaids, following some ancient sushi recipe, were wrapping his erect penis in seaweed. And just out of earshot, the unspeakable sound of behemoths rutting amongst the flotsam and jetsam of idioms, both dead and yet unborn. Somewhere, impossible worlds were being mapped, somehow — and there he was bound, on his bouncy bed, with his impossible words, stripy pyjamas and incarnadined buttocks. Shivering all over from sheer delight, he snuggled up under the eiderdown down, down…

'Are we all comfy now? Then I'll begin. Once upon a time…'

She paused for effect. He was hooked: reel him in.

'...there was a man called Zanzibar. Sostène Zanzibar. Just like you.'

Sostène was lurking at the far end of the gallery. He tried to picture himself *à rebours*, as though he were another, but failed to make the imaginative leap. A blinding flash of bald patch — the kind he occasionally glimpsed on surveillance monitors — was all he could conjure up: Friedrich's Wanderer with rampant alopecia. He squinted at the polished floorboards, and slowly looked up as the world unfolded, leaving him behind. He was James Stewart in *Vertigo*; Roy Scheider in *Jaws*. He was the threshold he could never cross. At the far end of the gallery Sostène was lurking.

Do you think she got the date wrong? said Yelena Moskovich. Encore un coup des gilets jaunes, said Cécile Guilbert. Could it be a publicity stunt? said Andrew Hodgson. Mais non, on n'est pas samedi, said Frédéric Beigbeder. Did she take a wrong turn at Crépy-en-Valois? said Adam Biles. Encore? said Virginie Despentes.

All eyes were on Lauren Ipsum, who had just arrived, fashionably late, at the lavish launch party for her debut collection of essays that straddled the porous border between criticism and autofiction. *Les yeux de merlan frit*, exquisitely translated by Victorine Gribiche for Editions de l'Olivier, had first been published, to great acclaim, by Fitzcarraldo Editions a few months prior, under the title *Fifty Shades of Grey Matter*. 'This seems to be the moment for the essay collection as memoir,' wrote Lara Feigel in *The Guardian*.

Smouldering behind a gold-tipped Sobranie, Lauren looked more glamorous than ever, in her crisp Clarice Lispector frock and speculative realist boots. Her neck was adorned with Oxfam pearls and love bites that resembled those little wild strawberries you happen upon by the roadside. She was standing among the crowd outside the gallery, one hand idling on the seat of Beigbeder's scooter (which was still warm), deep in conversation with Baek Jun-hwa, lead singer with The Ramens, a K-punk band from New Malden, who were scheduled to play a short set between the Q&A and the book signing session. Baek was a former member of The Knowing Eyebrows, Cretan Hop, Comma Splice, The Sixes and Sevens, The Isms, The Wordsmiths, Vehiculo Longo, The Intractable, The Nooks, The Dead Silence, The Stopped Clocks, The Penpushers, The Unknown, The Charles Shaw Appreciation Society, Musical Differences, The Crannies and, perhaps most famously, Cats Like Plain Crisps.

'*Marquise, vous n'êtes pas Ipsum pour des prunes,*' boomed Gabriel Josipovici before making a big show of kissing Lauren's hand in the manner of Mitteleuropa, interrupting a conversation which had meandered from Olivia Laing's pictures of pelargoniums on Instagram to the female camaraderie of cold-water swimming by way of Sally Rooney's pared-down turtlenecks and László Krasznahorkai's pop-up mint garden. 'Face it — you're neither young nor posh enough to write for the *New Statesman*,' someone said. 'I only read translations anyway,' someone else said. Sidonie de Nananaire rushed to greet her guest, brushing past Chloé Delaume, Josyane Savigneau, Joanna Walsh, Laurence Rémila, Fernando Sdrigotti, Annie Ernaux, Deborah Levy, and Nelly Kapriélian. Sostène charted the progress of her signature exploding bouffant across the gallery. A few minutes later, having ascertained that no one was watching, he followed in the footsteps of the self-styled *neo-rombière*.

'Allez ma chérie — mwah, mwah — tell us all about him,' said the hostess, 'on veut tout savoir. Tout.'

'Ladies,' said Lauren, brandishing a dick pic on her mobile, 'meet Rob Doyle, my new husband.'

They all went into raptures, gasping and mock-swooning like a shrill of schoolgirls.

'So what's he really like, underneath?' inquired Philiberte Moreau, when all the whooping had subsided. She increasingly resembled an approximation of one of her own doodles, and Lauren was unsure whether this was a good thing or not.

'Je ne vais pas énuméwer toutes ses qualités,' she replied, trying not to appear too cute with her Jane Birkin accent, 'mais je cwois que j'ai vwaiment de la chance.' She seemed to dwell on each word as though it were a world in which she might dwell. Forever.

Entranced, Sostène scrutinised his estranged wife from a safe distance. Like the past, she was another country now — out of bounds. She had returned herself to a place that precluded complete recognition. A place before them; before him, but mostly after. Sostène was rediscovering Lauren in her original strangeness, bathed in an otherworldly glow. This disquieting experience reminded him of standing outside his childhood home, as an adult, and feeling that he was haunting himself.

He was haunting himself again.

'Did you read the review?'

'C'est Yoko Ono là-bas?'

'Was it by Houman Barekat?'

'Mais non, c'est la nouvelle femme de machin.'

'Yes.'

'Houllebecq?'

'Most of them are these days.'

'Oui.'

'Yes.'

As soon as Lauren spotted Sostène, all the other women turned round and melted away, out of politeness or embarrassment. For a few seconds, they stood facing each other.

'Yes,' she said, breaking the ice with the same cruelty with which she had broken his heart, 'I do that bunny nose thing. And, yes, I put on a mean moose voice — so, sue me. I'm blessed with honeyed hair and bee-stung lips, and wear purple panties like no other. All that is a given I have taken away. When you look at me, your eyes light up like the 45,037 bulbs on the Plaza hotel in Las Vegas, where I wore a white see-through pencil skirt to our midnight wedding. Your heart still skips like a trip of jackrabbits in the Arizona desert, where we carved our names on a bench perilously close to the abyss. But when I look at you, well, I just feel dead inside. It has to be like this and no other way; otherwise it wouldn't be art, would it? Anyway, I was never quite all there, was I? Long before we met, I was a character in one of your stories — "Sweet Fanny Adams". A young man goes looking for the girl of his dreams in order to break up with her pre-emptively. "At last," he says upon meeting her, "I have found my sense of loss." See? I haven't forgotten. I started off as fiction, and to fiction I have returned. Our relationship was only a movement towards my disappearance. I am your sense of loss: the self-effacing subject of your work..."

'Lauren...' said Sostène.

'When you say my name, you retain nothing of me but my absence. And nobody is present behind these words I speak.'

And with these unwords she was gone. Lauren hailed a young waiter who was naked save for a polka dot bow tie. She picked a glass from the tray he bandied about with the recklessness of a seasoned tightrope walker. Her International Klein Blue eyes lingered on the departing buttocks as they threaded their way through the throng. She swished her drink around in the glass, absentmindedly. The waiter swayed to the cool clinking of the Zizek-shaped ice cubes. She swished some more.

Sidonie de Nananaire sidled up to her. 'Ton livre, ma chérie... En un mot: en-voû-tant. Ju-bi-la-toire. Et puis *tellement* subversif. Pierre-Jean has such good taste.'

Chiselled of chop and shiny of shoe, Pierre-Jean de Brissonneau was not one to be shushed lightly. He exuded natural authority. It was in his stature, posture, and ancestry; the cut of his suits and crispness of his shirts. It was in the size of his bank balance, the knobs on his timepieces and, above all, the bulge in his trousers. The latter was never openly acknowledged: like an eclipse, it could not be observed directly. The bulge was a given; its hegemonic presence always lurking in the background, just out of sight, or else glimpsed out of the corner of the eye — a black shape moving underwater. It hummed in unison with the air conditioning, an integral part of the ambient music of the publishing world. No, Pierre-Jean de Brissonneau was not one to be shushed lightly. He lorded it over editorial meetings with a patrician sense of entitlement everyone sensed he was entitled to. Mind you, he was a stickler for democracy, only imposing his own views once his colleagues had had ample opportunity to expose theirs. No, Pierre-Jean de Brissonneau really, really was not one to be shushed lightly. In fact, he was not one to be shushed at all. Yet shushed he had been, and nothing would ever be the same again. *Nothing.* Granted, it was not the loudest of shushes, not by a long chalk or any stretch of the imagination. More of a hush, really, if that. In truth, half a hush would probably cover it. And then some.

Yet this curt exhalation — this ill wind of change — had reverberated around the table like a violence without measure. Brissonneau played it over and over again in his mind, and each time it sounded more like a guillotine: shh! He began to wonder if it had not just been a loud sniffle, a muffled sneeze, or even a mere figment of his imagination. Confused, he made another attempt to get a word in edgeways, but the same young woman motioned him to hold his peace once more. The look of utter disbelief on his face was something to behold. He resembled Nicolae Ceausescu when his balcony speech was rudely interrupted by chanting, or Saddam Hussein's statue in Firdos Square, just before its toppling.

'Madame, I hear you are a very talented writer,' he said, 'but that's no excuse for…'

Lauren Ipsum raised a manicured index finger to her puckered lips before resuming her conversation with the man sitting to her right. Still in full flow, she unbuttoned her blouse and cupped a pert breast out of her scalloped brassiere. She let it defy gravity for a few minutes, while leafing through the thick brochure in front of her.

'Hang on, hang on… Ah, here's the passage!' she said,

and without even really looking, reached out and placed her hand on the back of Brissonneau's head, slowly bringing him level with her exposed mammary gland. Holding him tight by the scruff of the neck, she smeared his mouth across her nipple and round and round the areola. Thus embosomed, he had no other option but to suckle down at her teat. He did so greedily and soon closed his eyes.

'There, there,' she whispered, running her fingers through his thinning hair, 'all better now. Shh... Shh... Right. Where were we? Ah, yes, that passage on page 207...'

'In any event,' she said, doing her trademark bunny nose, 'you're not hard enough to take me up the bum.' By not she meant not ever. There was a finality to the sentence that left little room for interpretation. Sostène watched her pick some fluff off the pink roll-neck she had just folded on the bed. The double bed that might as well have been two singles. He wondered if a wife lost all respect for her husband as soon as the option of anal sex was removed from the equation. Perhaps it should always be lurking in the background, a mute reminder of the possibility of impossibility. That was in San Francisco.

On one of the corners of Rue des Abbesses and Rue Aristide Briand stands a café called La Villa. The decor could — and indeed shall — be described as gentlemen's club stroke colonial chic. African masks look down, with long Modigliani faces, from dark oak panelling. The lamps are always dimmed, as though some hallowed mystery had to be preserved from the cold light of day. In the first section, there are twelve black leather armchairs on either side of six black round tables. Sostène faces the armchair where Lauren once sat, with him, by the window. It is impossible to say for sure if it is the exact same one, or if the armchairs have been moved around. At bottom, it is a question of belief. Valentin believes, with every fibre of his being, that this is the armchair in which Lauren is no longer sitting. He believes that her behind is haunting the leather seat — that everything must leave some kind of mark, for fuck's sake. The distance separating the armchair in which Sostène is sitting from the luxury villa where Doyle is feeling Lauren's breasts and cunt is 787.2 kilometres. A distance, his mobile also informs him, that he could — and indeed shall — travel by car in seven hours and thirty-five minutes. He pinches out the screen repeatedly to magnify the satellite picture. He is a missile, zeroing in — past fields and forests — on the Med's answer to Southfork. Lauren slinks out to the pool in a sky-blue bikini and wide-brim sun hat, a slim volume dangling from her right hand. The distance separating the armchair in which Sostène is sitting from the armchair in which Lauren is no longer sitting is absolute. Sostène stands up and walks towards the empty armchair. 787.2 kilometres away, Doyle is feeling Lauren's breasts and cunt. In five steps, he should be there. Seven hours and thirty-five minutes away, Lauren slinks out to the pool in a sky-blue bikini and wide-brim sun hat, a slim volume dangling from her right hand. With each step, the café grows wider and the armchair recedes. The universe is expanding faster and faster, pushing everything away; tearing everyone apart.

When Sostène Zanzibar put pen to paper that day, he found it difficult to concentrate. His mind kept wandering, although no source of distraction was immediately detectable. No motorbikes mooing past down below. No high heels peppering the pavement with desire. No children shouting merry profanities on their way home from school. Yet his mind kept wandering, though he still knew not where. He focused on his mind focusing, but it did not seem to be going anywhere at all. Having drawn a blank — by applying layer upon layer of Tipp-Ex — he proceeded to make a point, until the nib of his pen had pierced the near virginal sheet of paper, which only a few crossed-out words had thus far desecrated. He picked up a printout of an e-mail Lauren had once sent him:
I LOVE YOU
I WANT YOU
I NEED YOU

I ADORE YOU
I MISS YOU
I AM OBSESSED WITH YOU
I ADMIRE YOU
I WORSHIP YOU
I CANNOT LIVE WITHOUT YOU

Having reread it, he reached for the Tipp-Ex:

I   YOU
I   YOU
I   YOU
I   YOU
I   YOU
I   YOU
I   YOU
I   YOU
I   YOU

The universe was expanding, tearing them apart.

Are those spots of blood he spots on her riding breeches? Not spots per se, perhaps, or even — upon closer inspection — spots at all, for that matter, which is not to say, of course, that the breeches are ipso facto spotless. Far from it, in fact. Spot-free, yes, probably — *possibly* — but not spotless, no, on account of those flecks — or are they spots? — all down the inside of her left thigh. Was any cupping involved, he wonders? Did his testes roll around in her hand like wine in a taster's palate? If so, was that before slipping on her latex gloves? Did she apply a little pressure at any point, possibly towards the end? Did it remind him of the way she squeezes the bulb on her vintage atomiser? Did he reflect, however briefly, upon the transformation of liquid into fine spray? Did he marvel, if only for a split second, at that small miracle? Did he picture her in a mist of musk and black silk stockings? At what stage did she place her left foot on the milking stool? Was that before slipping on her latex gloves? Did she assume this position on practical or aesthetic grounds? Was it a bit of both? Did he read anything into it, and if not, why not? Did he think, on reflection, that he should have done, and if so, why? Would he say that the adoption of this posture accounts (at least in part) for the presence of those spots (or flecks) on her riding breeches? Was it, shall we say, a contributory factor? Did he witness the appearance of a pattern on her left thigh? Was it like a slowly exposed action painting caught on Polaroid? Was it like a time-lapse of a newborn's features morphing, over the years, into a death mask? Is the corpse the truth of the biological individual? Was it at this juncture that she slipped on her latex gloves? And what were they doing on the floor in the first place?

Lauren Ipsum went out at seven. It could have been at six, of course, or even at five; indeed it usually was. That day, however, it was at seven, on account of her husband being frightfully late. Consistent is the life he leads, trilled the maid, who often likened him to the ever punctual pater familias in *Mary Poppins*. You could set the time by his comings and goings; indeed everybody did. At five o' clock sharp, the maid would start dusting, scrubbing, mopping and ironing as if propelled by the velocity of a hard day's work. At five on the dot, Lauren Ipsum — freshly abluted and made up — stood poised to greet her husband like a domestic goddess who would never dream of spending the afternoon in the company of young bell boys with the stamina of Duracell bunnies. No, it really was not like him at all, said the maid, shaking her head; totally out of character. Lost in thought, Lauren Ipsum gazed out of the window, blinking into the blinding light that was streaming in. She was fiddling with her pearl necklace as if it were a rosary. You always know where you are with him, said the maid. *And what about without him?* Lost tout court, Lauren Ipsum gazed out of the window, blinking into the blinding light that was streaming in from long, long ago. *I have seen the light and now I cannot see.* She was fiddling with her pearl necklace as if rolling testicles around between thumb and forefinger. Her late husband was in fact so late now that it could only be too late. Dinner would be ruined.

Seven hours and thirty-five minutes later, Lauren slunk out to the pool in a sky-blue bikini and wide-brim sun hat. She screamed, dropping a slim volume by Raymond Roussel into the water. Sostène was standing there, holding a notebook. He raised his index finger to his lips, then whispered: 'I will cause you to be absent'. He opened the notebook and wrote This Woman over and over again.

When he finally looked up, she had disappeared. Sostène felt tired after driving 787.2 kilometres. He walked into the villa and fell asleep on a leather sofa. There he dreamt that Lauren was pregnant with his novel.

'It's been in here for more than nine months,' she said pointing to her belly, 'but the bloody thing won't come out.'

He woke up still sleeping to find himself in bed, wearing his stripy pyjamas. Lauren tucked him in, picked up a big picture book and started reading out loud:

'Once upon a time…'

She paused for effect. He was hooked.

'…there was a man called Sostène. Sostène Zanzibar. Just like you. He thought he was haunted by a ghost, but his ex wife assured him that there was no such thing. "There are no ghosts," she said. "There are no ghosts".'

Sostène opened his eyes. He was all alone, but Lauren's voice was still ringing in his ears. There are no ghosts, there are no ghosts, there are no ghosts, there are no ghosts…

ERIC GIRAUDET DE BOUDEMANGE

Grans et hideus a desmesure,
Issi tres laide creature
Qu'en ne porroit dire de bouche,
Illuec seoit seur une couche,
Une grant machue en se main.

nmense et hideux à l'extrême,
ref, une créature si laide
u'on ne saurait l'exprimer en paroles,
ait là, assis sur une souche,
ne grande massue à la main.
e m'approchai du rustre,

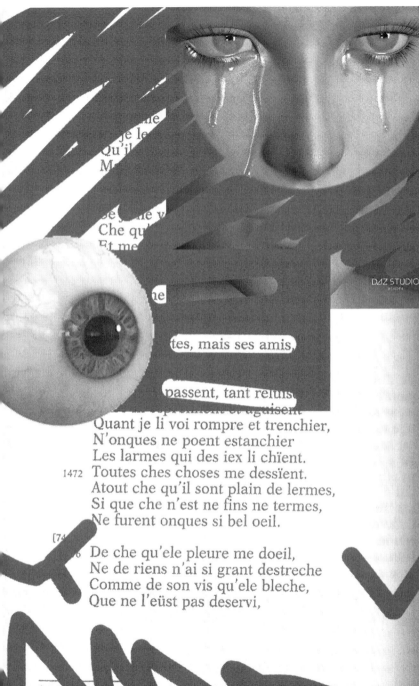

tes, mais ses amis,

passent, tant reluis

Quant je li voi rompre et trenchier,
N'onques ne poent estanchier
Les larmes qui des iex li chïent.
1472 Toutes ches choses me dessïent.
Atout che qu'il sont plain de lermes,
Si que che n'est ne fins ne termes,
Ne furent onques si bel oeil.

De che qu'ele pleure me doeil,
Ne de riens n'ai si grant destreche
Comme de son vis qu'ele bleche,
Que ne l'eüst pas deservi,

---

* 1452. [...] (ou [...] d'apr. [...] mss.) 1460. je meisme [...] err. a [...] les mss. [...] se p[...]

** 1449. Des [...] ele entor lui se tret *V*; Des [...] le a[...] l'a tret (*ou* l'atret) *H* 1451. si l'ole (*mss.*) 1454. Qu'encor a. *V*; Toz jorz a[...] 1465. rien t. *mss.* 1468. D'ire m'angoissent *GV*

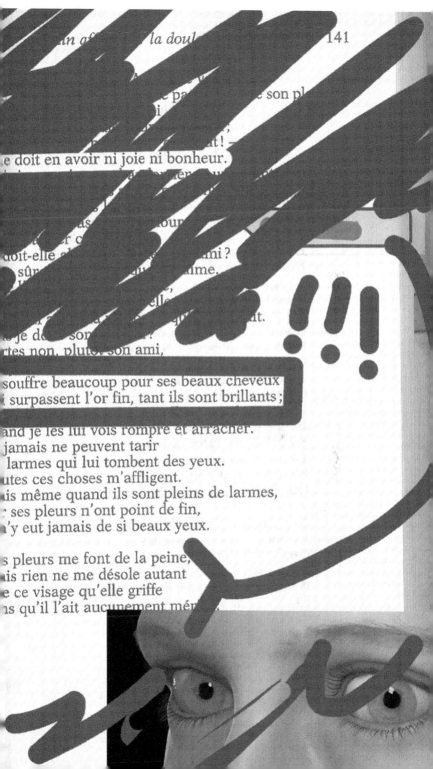

141

e doit en avoir ni joie ni bonheur.

doit-elle

tes non, plutôt son ami,

souffre beaucoup pour ses beaux cheveux
surpassent l'or fin, tant ils sont brillants ;

and je les lui vois rompre et arracher.
jamais ne peuvent tarir
larmes qui lui tombent des yeux.
utes ces choses m'affligent.
is même quand ils sont pleins de larmes,
ses pleurs n'ont point de fin,
'y eut jamais de si beaux yeux.

s pleurs me font de la peine,
is rien ne me désole autant
e ce visage qu'elle griffe
is qu'il l'ait aucunement mér

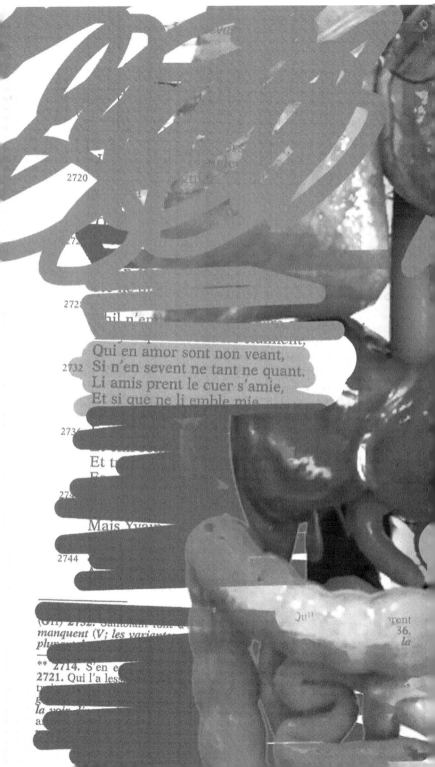

2720

2728

     il n'en

     Qui en amor sont non veant,
2732 Si n'en sevent ne tant ne quant.
     Li amis prent le cuer s'amie,
     Et si que ne li emble mie,

2736

     Et t

     Mais Yv

2744

manquent (V; les variant
plu

** 2714. S'en e
2721. Qui l'a les

était perfide, séducteur et vo...
Ce voleur a séduit ma dame,
ui ne soupçonnait guère la moindre perfidie,
qui ne croyait pas qu'il dût, pour rien au monde,

ain, lui, a tué ma dame,
r elle lui a dit de lui garder
n cœur et de le lui rapporter
ant que l'année ne fût écoulée.

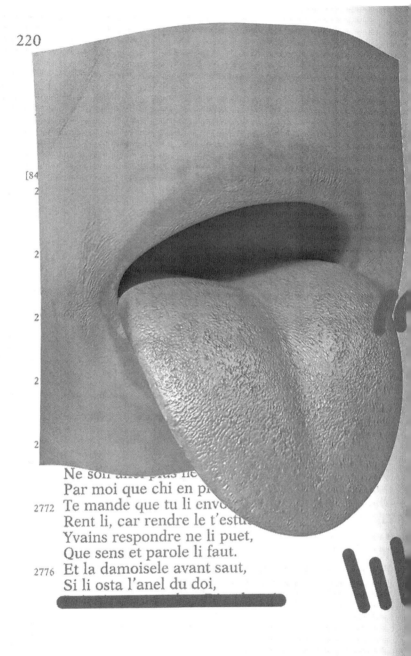

Ne soit aine plus ne
Par moi que chi en p[...]
2772 Te mande que tu li envo[...]
Rent li, car rendre le t'est[...]
Yvains respondre ne li puet,
Que sens et parole li faut.
2776 Et la damoisele avant saut,
Si li osta l'anel du doi,

---

* 2746. m. fu (*HV*) 2758. n. tourne et retourne (*mauvaise rime*; SH) 2759. Et l. j.; *second qui manque* (*mss.*) 2762. Ni sui p. (*HGV*) 2763. Car vous ai trouve a sejour (*leçon unique*; VH)

** 2747. t. pot *mss.* 2750. la feste S. J. *mss.* 2757-58. *intervertis* H 2760-61. Ensi li leal a. f./contre l. t. *H* 2765-66. gabez nous as/Ma dame quant tu l'esposas *G*; trais nous as/Qui a ma dame trespassas *S*

La messagère réclame

OUBLIANS

...ain, tu as donc bien perdu la mémoire,
...i qui n'as pas pu te souvenir
...e tu aurais dû revenir
...près de ma dame au bout de l'an :
...est jusqu'à la fête de la Saint-Jean
...'elle te donna comme délai.

...ais tu l'as tenue en tel mépris
...e tu ne t'es plus souvenu d'elle.
...a dame a fait peindre sur les murs de sa chambre
...us les jours et toutes les saisons,
...r la personne qui aime reste absorbée dans ses pensé...
... loin de pouvoir prendre un bon som...
...ute la nuit elle dénombre et additio...e
.... et qui s'en vont.
...is-tu comment font les amants ?
...comptent le passage du temps et de chaque saison.
... plainte ne se p..........
...un jour trop tôt.
...urtant je ne parle pas pour faire une réclamation en
...ut ce que je te dis, c'est que celle qui te fit   [jus...
...ouser ma dame nous a trahis.
...ain, ma dame désormais ne se soucie plus de toi ;
...i plus est, elle te commande, par mon intermédiaire,
... ne jamais revenir auprès d'elle
... de ne pl.. garder son anneau.
...est par moi que tu vois ici devant toi,
...'elle t'ordonne de le lui envoyer.

...ain ne peut lui répondre,
...r le sens et la parole lui font défaut.
... demoiselle, elle, s'élance vers lui
... lui ôte l'anneau du doigt ;

ANDREW HODGSON
Tuileries

Therefore, that is to say. Well, nothing much more when, that morning we'd stood on opposing platforms at Tuileries and you faintly held up a hand, or not morning, not yet morning. Quite. Not. Watch the hand and station disappear off altogether, blur out until it is my own still hand, raised, I see there. Reflected. And, soaked toe to tip, I and Claude go east, to change at Rambuteau. The train rather than gear, and, eleven, to République and he to his coloc and I my. For clothes to dry the night, the morning, as we had no others. And you and Margaux there, too much –

And Caroline and Margaux there, out west off to Pont d'Alma a last time, where they lived in that granny flat that, rented directly off the cat who called it home and had outlasted said granny, always stank of piss. Have to rip out the walls, redo the plaster, heard say. People. But, some sick joke or, the apartment comes with the cat, mesdames. The animal is legally your propriétaire, and, okay. And, I guess they packed the last of their one bag they together lived out of and to the airport. I guess. Change of clothes, and never did see them again. And, I wonder, now and then, if anyone ever fed the cat, after that.

But how was it that we met, I don't – on the canal, by Cork and Cavan there where, beers, from the alimentation rather than from the naff bar itself. Outside by, but that's not it. But, on the canal there, and, that'll have to be enough. Close enough, to start. You, she, Caroline, I mean –

Caroline sat, though Margaux and Claude and all that: 'is it 17h30 already? She's always so late,' she went. And, 'aye,' and 'Claude and all, everyone.' And we'd sat, and talked, a bit. A while. Not that we had before. Something else. I don't think, because there and then the tension as if we hadn't. Perhaps we had. And Caroline took the bottle caps from the floor where we'd flicked them and, wrapped in a curved index and stabilised, a slight, by thumb, skimmed the first, three before it washed away below the water, and the second not at all, and I said you're littering, I said

'that's littering.'

And, whatever, they dredge it, she said, for bicycles and washing machines, and bodies, whatever –

And it was 2h, about that, next morning in Truskel by

Grand Boulevards where we'd sat, altogether now, as Claude and Margaux et al. came by eventually, on the église-style benches that run the wall over by the nook. Benches under where we kept the boxes of bottles, because who pays, why pay. Pour them out into other people's glasses. Leave the boxes of empties there, under bench, when we leave around 4h. For the bar staff to find in clean up, but – I mean, who was sat in that nook that night anyway? And Caroline and I had stood to research the fumoir in the basement, pushed through the dancefloor and the spiral steps on the other side of the salle, by the bar there and down into the cav boxed off in glass, set off by vast extraction fans that did little to dispel the smoke sat upon the few dozen bodies wedged there, fuming.

Smoked straights, then, as before taxes came in. And so no one stood with packets of fleur du pays, filtres, ephemera, nor feuille stuck to lip as speaking, as fumoirs now taken up for jockeying space, for elbow room. But pressed up, against the glass, and a dozen other people Caroline goes that she's leaving tomorrow, and, fair, and she says to, to –

And pressed up against one other, against the glass, against a dozen other people only the whirrs of the extraction fans and the dull bub of voices mélanging and nothing much else, and she reaches, Caroline, out a hand

and pulls on the buttons on my shirt, that were a kind of faux-mother of pearl, I think. Because, fancy. Ish. As the fumers fumed and swayed this and that in cycle, unstable. Circadian. Probably not. And her face sort of dropped as she spoke and no sound reached me, really. Not really. A whirring. Hubbub. Tidal. Probably not. And she let her hand come away, and back vaguely to her side as the shift died down, and well. And, inappropriate, really, to ask for clarity. For, répéter what she had said, for why. S'il te plait. Just so. And so, 'fair, it'll be great, that place is great.' I don't know, what else, hein ?

And 4h30, or so, after the larger group I have only lightly let here enter in vague inference tapers off, and I and C, and C and M, made our way from the alleys and dog shit, to the curated river, with the lights, for C and M to say bye. To generate a memory of saying bye, as in the morning they'd pack their one bag, and pour out the sack of cat feed, I guess, and off, to the airport, terminal something and off and out to – Down along the boulevard past Lafayette, and cup the back of Opéra, to Pyramides along, above ground, that is. And, at the gardens laid out before the Louvre, Margaux goes piss in the entry to the Tuileries hedge maze and we the rest sit and talk on, nothing I guess, as the image of the mouths moving there repeat in gif, kick the gravel, open bottles. But no rasp or words or chinking glass, that's all gone before,

'Fuck sake !'

As M falls out from the hedges, scraping shit off her shoe along the kerb there. And, human this time. Human shit, and ponders aloud whether it was due to the late night cruising for which the mazes there are traditionally put to use, or desperate tourists from the queue to photograph the Mona Lisa. Attrition. The queue. War of. The queue.

And the smell lingered, as we pass onto the rive droite, and M takes off her shoes, to throw in the Seine. Joking, like. But, miscalculated off they go, and stood there at the lip of the brick incline onto its surface, the Seine, watch them float, a bit, and then wash away under water. But visible, still, unlike everything else. As only shallow. So human-chain down to the river, and trousers rolled because, 'it's only a couple feet deep, I reckon.' I reckon, but its not, and to waist to fish out them out, to leave on the bank. And again, left there, when we leave. Soon enough after. From the rive droite.

But in the water, all four now. To chest, just about. To swim through the orange ripples refracted off the uplit buildings and decorative streetlamps, off Orsay and that, yellow, where the clock face stands. Around the top, just above the names of city stations to which it no longer connects, above the window from which that train once crashed out to street. Over there, yeah. For serious. Saw the photo, Caroline reckons. Maybe. And Claude doing lengths out in the middle of the river, and you, Caroline wraps her legs and arms around me, I kicking water, just about. Not all that well, just about. And kicking not all that well really, I pushed down under water and find no floor, but arms and hands out sprouting from deep below, billowing this way and that down there, twisting about my feet and push you off me, to make surface, and spit the water out. And heave, a bit. A lot. But you're already gone. On the bank there, with Margaux, and,

'You know the sewers empty right out into the river, right ? You fucking tramps.'

Goes M. And,

'Oh, right.'

To make land, and wait, a minute. Watch debris block light in the slight waves and wonder if it's human. Spit some more, though the taste of drain doesn't really go anywhere really. Remains there, the next day. A while.

But walk silent now, with Caroline and listen to M and C talk this and that I no longer recall, to the métro, where they open the grills as we wait, laid across by the steps, nearly morning. Nearly. And down into the tunnels, and jump the barriers because, who pays. Why –

~And, a sort of, collective exhale, and passive 'ciao,' as we filter out to east and west and stand there, filtered out on opposing platforms, and the train, our train, my and Claude's train chunters in, and between us. And I stand, in the full-length glass window of the far doors unused, and you kind of purse your lips and squint, a little, and you raise a hand in open palm to which I mimic, and watch the hand, the station wash away, before quickly. Soon enough quickly, it is I framed there in the mirror of that unused doorway.

PHILIPP TIMISCHL

The feeling in Paris is very expensive.

CONTRIBUTORS

Camille Bloomfield, alias Campo, travaille la voix sous toutes ses formes ou presque : en poésie, souvent ; en performance, parfois ; en chant et slam, de plus en plus. Spécialiste de la littérature à contraintes (Oulipo) et fan de poésie expérimentale, faisant dès qu'elle le peut des incursions dans le hip hop et la soul, elle est aussi co-fondatrice de l'Outranspo, un collectif qui pratique la traduction créative. Sa poésie et sa musique sont nées sur les réseaux sociaux, dégenrées & libérées des catégorisations académiques. Attirée par tout ce qui touche au collectif, ses performances sont souvent participatives // camillebloomfield.com // instagram : @clebilingue

Amalie Brandt is an artist and curator living and working in Paris.

Chris Clarke was raised in Western Canada, and currently lives in Philadelphia. His published translations include work by Pierre Mac Orlan (Wakefield Press), and Oulipo members Raymond Queneau (New Directions),

François Caradec (MIT Press), Olivier Salon and Jacques Jouet (Toad Press). His translation of Marcel Schwob's *Imaginary Lives* (Wakefield Press) was awarded the 2019 French-American Foundation Translation Prize, an award for which his translation of Nobel Prize winner Patrick Modiano's *In the Café of Lost Youth* (NYRB Classics) was a finalist in 2017. A doctoral candidate in French at the Graduate Center, CUNY, his dissertation examines the role of translation in the career of French novelist Raymond Queneau.

Gaia Di Lorenzo (b. Rome 1991) is a visual artist. She graduated in Literature and Philosophy from the University of Tor Vergata and then with honours in Fine Arts, from Goldsmiths University of London. Since 2013 she has been writing about contemporary art and aesthetics on "Tempo Presente", a magazine founded by Ignazio Silone in 1956. Gaia considers the following curatorial activities as part of her artistic practice (both as research and product) as it is deeply routed in collaboration and reactivity. In 2014 she founded the project SHIFT: an artistic organisation that was responsible for planning exhibitions of international artists based in London. The aim of the project was to encourage artists to produce work as a reaction to a context . For this reason the chosen exhibition spaces had a strong character and not only were they not "white cubes" but they were not related at all to contemporary art. In 2015 she organised an artistic residence in Ansedonia, Tuscany. The 16 artists were invited to use the time as an opportunity to gather material and give life to spontaneous and possibly ephemeral artworks. Gaia's latest project is CASTRO (Contemporary Art STudios ROme): a space for artistic learning and production in Rome. The project offers studio spaces to artists and curators selected via an open application system; the public program is also a rally point for the wider artistic community. The program encourages criticality as a strategy for the production of knowledge. It promotes an experimental and highly collaborative learning model. In 2017 she was nominated as finalist for the Menabrea Award. Among her most recent exhibitions are: "Sitting Amongst" at Jupiter Woods, London; "An Entertainment in Conversation and Verse" curated by Maria Adele Del Vecchio at Tiziana Di Caro Gallery, Naples; "Goldsmiths Degree Show" in London. Upcoming is her solo show at ADA Gallery in Rome. Her contribution here is -as is her consuetude- a collection of references coupled with her own response to them. The work is deeply influenced by her most recent conversations with the writer Allison Grimaldi- Donahue.

Craig Dworkin is the author, most recently, of *Chapter XXIV* (Red Butte Press, 2013), *Alkali*

(Counterpath Press, 2015), *12 Erroneous Displacements and a Fact* (Information As Material, 2016), and *DEF* (Information As Material, 2017); he serves as founding curator of the Eclipse collection (eclipsearchive.org).

Lauren Elkin is the author most recently of *Flâneuse: Women Walk the City*. She writes in French and English, and lives in Paris and Liverpool.

Andrew Gallix is an Anglo-French writer and freelance journalist. His work has appeared in the *Guardian*, *Financial Times*, *Irish Times*, *New Statesman*, *Independent*, *Literary Review*, *Times Literary Supplement*, *Dazed & Confused*, *BBC Radio 3* and elsewhere. He teaches at Sorbonne Université (Paris IV) and divides his time between Scylla and Charybdis.

Eric Giraudet de Boudemange (EGdB) starts with field work, an ethnographic experience that he brings to the studio. His "stories" take different shapes: sculpture, performance, video, and recently a video game. They often talk about history, folk & pop culture, and biology with a taste for absurdist British humour.
His participation for the « Paris book » is part of an artwork to be played: *Yvain!*, developed in collaboration with game designer Tomavatars and produced by La

Criée, centre d'art contemporain in Rennes. The pages of the bilingual edition novel (a mix of vernacular dialects from Champagne and Picardie, and contemporary french) float in the 3D experimental adventure game. The piece is inspired by a passage from the novel *Yvain, the Knight to the Lion* by Chrétien de Troyes, written in the twelfth century. Heartbroken, Yvain the knight flees civilization. He sinks into the forest, leaving his clothes, losing the use of speech and reason. In this contemporary interpretation, we guide the main character, at the paste of his lament, through an absurd and offbeat medieval universe, at the crossroads of courtly love and *Game of Thrones*. You can download the game for free on https://la-criee.itch.io/yvain

Andrew Robert Hodgson (b. Hull, 1988) is author of the novels *Reperfusion* (WPS&B, 2012) and *Mnemic Symbols* (Dostoyevsky Wannabe, 2019), the monograph *The Post-War Experimental Novel: British and French Fiction, 1945 – 1975* (Bloomsbury, 2019), and editor of this experimental writing collection, *Paris* (Dostoyevsky Wannabe, 2019). He is translator from the French of Roland Topor's *Head-to-Toe Portrait of Suzanne* (Atlas Press, 2018) and from the Danish, Carl Julius Salomonsen's *New Forms of Art and Contagious Mental Illness* (New Documents, 2019). He is Teaching and Research Fellow in British literature at Université Paris Est.

Stewart Home is an award-winning visual artist and the author of 15 novels, 7 works of cultural commentary, 1 collection of stories and 1 collection of poetry. His most recent book is *Re-Enter The Dragon: Genre Theory, Brucesploitation & the Sleazy Joys of Lowbrow Cinema* (2018). Home was born and lives in London. When he isn't shredding copies of his own books as live art, he likes to entertain audiences by standing on his head spewing obscenities. Website:
https://www.stewarthomesociety.org/
Twitter: @stewarthome1

Ian Monk was born near London, but now lives in Paris, where he works as a writer and translator (of, among others, Georges Perec, Raymond Roussel and Jacques Roubaud). After contributing to the *Oulipo Compendium* (Atlas Press) he became a member of the Oulipo in 1988. He has published books in English such as *Family Archaeology* and *Writings for the Oulipo* (Make Now), in French (*Plouk Town* and *Là* (Cambourakis)), and even both languages *N/S* (with Frédéric Forte) and *Les Feuilles de Yucca / Leaves of the Yucca*, a bilingual ebook (www.contre-mur.com/). A new collection of his French poetry *Vers de l'infini* has recently been published by Cambourakis.

Yelena Moskovich is a Ukrainian-born (USSR), American and French artist and writer, author of *Virtuoso* and *The Natashas* (Serpent's Tail, 2019, 2016). Her plays and performances have been produced in the US, Vancouver, Paris, and Stockholm. Her fiction has won the Gallery Beggar Press Short Story Prize in 2016 and has been featured in *Dyke On Magazine*, and *The Skirt Chronicles*. She has also written for *The Paris Review*, *New Statesman*, *3:AM Magazine*, *Happy Reader*, and *Mixte Magazine*. In 2018, she was served as one of the curators and exhibiting artists of the Queer Biennial Los Angeles.

Olivier Salon has been a member of the Oulipo since 2000, he is a writer (poetry, theatre, short stories), a mathematician (hmm, hmm, used to be), an alpinist (he climbed twice El Capitan, in the Yosemite Park, and wrote his adventure in the book *El Capitan*), a pianist, and an actor (several pieces around Oulipo texts, as *Pièces détachées*, *Chant'Oulipo* (Oulipo songs) and *Conference in the shape of pear* (devoted to Erik Satie)).

When the moon is full, he plays the piano in the company of werewolves.

Olivier Salon's bio, rendered in verse form using only the letters of his name, by **Harry Matthews**:

Raise all veils!

Loose all reins! Learn a real lesson,

See a vision alive,

A lover's roll, sails all aroil.

Role:

Revive senses (never seen),

Release lines, veins, violins.

Rinse all lenses (& leave vile ones alone),

Serene, involve all reason, loose on all airs

Verve & verses on a run.

Alive! alive

In one lore.

Philipp Timischl, born in 1989, is an Austrian artist currently living and working in Vienna. His practice spans various media such as video, sculpture, painting and photography, often combined with text and culminating in site-specific installations. A reoccurring theme in his work is power dynamics – often in relation to social classes, queerness, heritage and the art world.

Typographers Note:

As part of Dostoyevsky Wannabe's increasing interest in documenting the design and the typographical form of the books that we produce, decisions made regarding typography in this volume, where possible, weigh heavily towards the individual wishes of the contributors and not necessarily towards typical typographical conventions.

Typeset by Dostoyevsky Wannabe Design in Sabon LT Pro with Lato display.

Printed in Great Britain
by Amazon